"I need to find my daughter." If Quinn could find a scent trail, they might be able to follow it to Boyd's location.

"You need to slow down, Captain."

"That's an easy thing to say when it's not your daughter in the hands of a serial killer," Justin responded, regretting it immediately. He knew Gretchen cared deeply about the work she did and about the people she worked for.

"Maybe. Probably. But we have a job to do here, and the first step in that is figuring out where he took her."

"That's what Quinn and I are going to do. Find!" he commanded and the Malinois took off, sprinting downstairs and out the door. Sirens were blaring, lights flashing on the pavement. Backup was there, but Justin ignored everything but his K-9 partner.

* * *

MILITARY K-9 UNIT:

These soldiers track down a serial killer
with the help of their brave canine partners.

Mission to Protect–Terri Reed, April 2018
Bound by Duty–Valerie Hansen, May 2018
Top Secret Target–Dana Mentink, June 2018
Standing Fast–Maggie K. Black, July 2018
Rescue Operation–Lenora Worth, August 2018
Explosive Force–Lynette Eason, September 2018
Battle Tested–Laura Scott, October 2018
Valiant Defender–Shirlee McCoy, November 2018
Military K-9 Unit Christmas–Valerie Hansen and
Laura Scott, December 2018

Aside from her faith and her family, there's not much **Shirlee McCoy** enjoys more than a good book! When she's not teaching or chauffeuring her five kids, she can usually be found plotting her next Love Inspired Suspense story or wandering around the beautiful Inland Northwest in search of inspiration. Shirlee loves to hear from readers. If you have time, drop her a line at shirlee@shirleemccoy.com.

Books by Shirlee McCoy

Love Inspired Suspense

Military K-9 Unit

Valiant Defender

FBI: Special Crimes Unit

Night Stalker
Gone

Mission: Rescue

Protective Instincts
Her Christmas Guardian
Exit Strategy
Deadly Christmas Secrets
Mystery Child
The Christmas Target
Mistaken Identity
Christmas on the Run

Classified K-9 Unit

Bodyguard

Visit the Author Profile page at Harlequin.com for more titles.

Valiant Defender

Shirlee McCoy

HARLEQUIN® LOVE INSPIRED® SUSPENSE

Special thanks and acknowledgment are given to Shirlee McCoy for her contribution to the Military K-9 Unit miniseries.

Recycling programs for this product may not exist in your area.

ISBN-13: 978-1-335-54409-4

Valiant Defender

This edition published by arrangement with Love Inspired Books.

www.Harlequin.com

Printed in U.S.A.

How excellent is thy lovingkindness, O God! therefore the children of men put their trust under the shadow of thy wings. They shall be abundantly satisfied with the fatness of thy house; and thou shalt make them drink of the river of thy pleasures. For with thee is the fountain of life: in thy light shall we see light.

–*Psalms* 36:7-9

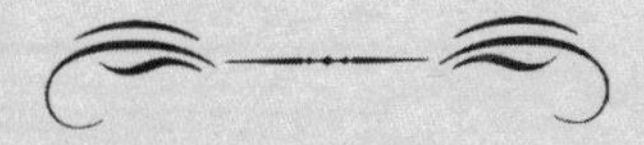

To my continuity buddies,
Dana, Laura, Lenora, Lynette, Mags, Terri and Val, with much affection and admiration. And, most especially, to Emily, who puts up with all our writing shenanigans.

ONE

Canyon Air Force Base was silent. Houses shuttered, lights off. Streets quiet. Just the way it should be in the darkest hours of the morning. Captain Justin Blackwood didn't let the quiet make him complacent. Seven months ago, an enemy had infiltrated the base. Boyd Sullivan, aka the Red Rose Killer—a man who'd murdered five people in his hometown before he'd been caught—had escaped from prison and continued his crime spree, murdering several more people and wreaking havoc on the base. He'd released two hundred highly trained military dogs from the base kennel and created a feeling of unease among the community. Sullivan wanted to destroy everyone and everything that he blamed for his failures.

Justin planned to stop him.

"What are your thoughts, Captain?" Captain Gretchen Hill asked as he sped through the quiet community. A temporary transfer from Minot Air Force Base, Gretchen had been in Texas for several months, observing the way Justin, himself a K-9 handler, commanded the Security Forces. When she returned to her post, she'd help set up a K-9 unit there.

"I don't think we're going to find him at the house," he responded. "But when it comes to Boyd Sullivan, I believe in checking out every lead."

"The witness reported lights? She didn't actually see Boyd?"

"She didn't see him, but the family that lived in the house left for a new post two days ago. Lots of moving trucks and activity. She's worried Sullivan might have noticed and decided to squat in the empty property. Since she lives on the same court, she's terrified."

"Based on how easily Boyd has slipped through our fingers these past few months, I'd say he's too smart to squat in base housing," Gretchen said.

"I agree," Justin responded. He'd been surprised at how much he enjoyed working with Gretchen. He'd expected her presence to feel like a burden, one more person to worry about and protect. But she had razor-sharp intellect and a calm, focused demeanor that had been an asset to the team. She didn't shirk duties, didn't complain about long hours, didn't stand back and take notes while others did the job. She'd thrown herself into her temporary assignment wholeheartedly.

As much as Justin had dreaded her arrival, he was going to miss her when she was gone.

"Even if he decided to spend a few nights in an empty house, why turn on the lights? He knows this base. He knows that everyone on it is on high alert and searching for him."

"If he's there, he wants us to know it," Justin responded. It was the only explanation that made sense. And it was the kind of game Sullivan liked to play—taunting his intended victims, letting them know that he was closing in. He left red roses and notes before he struck. *I'm coming for you.* He loved to kill, but terrorizing people was his drug of choice.

He needed to be stopped.

Tonight. Not in another month or two or three.

For the sake of the people on base and for Portia's sake.

Just thinking about his sixteen-year-old daughter being targeted by Sullivan made Justin's blood run cold. A year and a half ago, Portia had come to live with him unexpectedly and reluctantly, forced to give up her school and friends after her mother died in a car accident. The loss had hit her hard. A shy teenager who seemed to have trouble connecting with her peers, she'd turned to the internet for comfort and amused herself by blogging. Unfortunately, she'd chosen the wrong topic, and had been unmasked as the anonymous blogger on the Red Rose Killer.

She'd had no idea, of course, that Justin and Boyd had crossed paths long before Boyd's escape from prison. She'd had no idea just how much danger she was putting herself in.

While Justin and his team had struggled to find Boyd and identify the anonymous blogger, Portia had been quietly listening to their conversations and gathering information that she'd posted online. Worse, she'd mocked Boyd—a man who was as arrogant as he was dangerous. That, along with being Justin's daughter, had put her in the crosshairs of the killer. She'd received a threatening note from Boyd a week ago, and that terrified Justin.

If anything happened to Portia, Justin would never forgive himself.

Please, Lord, help me keep her safe.

The prayer flitted through his mind as he turned into a cul-de-sac and eyed the darkened windows of the houses there. This was the quiet residential area of the base. Single-family homes that housed the larger families of airmen and officers.

"It's the brick two-story, right?" Gretchen asked, leaning forward as he approached the house.

"Yes."

"And our witness was certain of what she saw?"

"Yes. She said the house was lit up like a beacon. Almost every room in it. She noticed when she brought her dog out for a walk. Her husband is deployed, and she didn't want to check it out herself, so she called it in."

"It could have been a cleaning crew. That is a nice-size house, and there are plenty of air force personnel with big families who'd love to have it. I doubt it's going to stay empty long," Gretchen suggested as Justin pulled into the driveway of the two-story brick home. Currently there were no lights in any of the windows. The front door was closed, as were all the visible windows. Someone may have been there, but the place looked empty now.

"That thought crossed my mind, but I want to check it out, anyway." He turned off the engine, and his K-9, Quinn, shifted impatiently in his travel crate. The Belgian Malinois loved his work, and he was anxious to get out and do it. Trained in suspect apprehension, he had a great nose and a strong prey-and-play drive that made him easy to train and a pleasure to work with. When they'd first been partnered together, Quinn had reminded Justin of Scout—a German shepherd he'd found as a puppy and fostered until he was old enough to enter the K-9 training program. At the time, Justin already had a K-9 partner. Scout had been partnered with another officer and earned a reputation for being a superstar on the team, but he'd remained one of Justin's favorite dogs.

Now he was missing, along with two more of the four superstar German shepherds that had been released from the kennels by Sullivan.

"Ready, boy?" Justin asked his K-9 as he climbed out of the SUV.

Quinn shifted again, whining softly.

"What's the plan?" Gretchen asked, following him to the back of the SUV.

"Quinn and I will do a perimeter search. He'll know if someone is here."

"You and Quinn? And I'm supposed to wait here and twiddle my thumbs?"

"You are going to keep your eye on the

front door. I don't want anyone escaping out the front while Quinn and I are around back."

"Come on, Captain. You know that's not going to happen."

"When it comes to Boyd Sullivan, I know we need to expect the unexpected." He opened Quinn's crate and hooked the dog to his leash.

"When it comes to Sullivan, you'd be happy if you could keep everyone away from him. Admit it. You want me to stay here so I don't get anywhere close to the guy we're after."

She was right, but he wasn't going to argue the validity of his feelings. The fact was, he was Boyd's target, and he didn't want Gretchen to be collateral damage. "Stay here, Captain."

He headed around the side of the house, Quinn heeling beside him. The dog was nearly prancing with excitement, his nose in the air, his tail high.

And Gretchen, of course, was following, her boots thudding softly on the grassy side yard.

"I told you to stay with the vehicle," he said, not glancing in her direction. His focus was ahead—the dark backyard and shadowy corners.

"Unfortunately for you, we're of equal rank and equal authority. This is your base, so usually I do things your way, but going into a situation like this without backup is dangerous. So, this time, I'm doing things my way," she said, and he couldn't argue. If Boyd weren't a factor, he wouldn't have told her to stay at the SUV.

They were both well-trained military police officers.

They'd both reached the rank of captain.

She was as capable as Justin.

He was still worried.

Quinn turned a tight circle at the corner of the house, his ears twitching, his scruff raised.

He'd caught a scent. Justin released him from the leash.

"Find," he commanded, and Quinn barked once, excited. Eager. He bounded toward the back door of the house, head high, obviously detecting a scent.

Please, God, let it be Boyd, Justin prayed silently.

He wanted this over. He wanted Boyd behind bars, his victims finally receiving the justice they deserved, their families finally receiving closure.

Portia safe.

Quinn snuffled an old mat that had been left near the back door, turned a quick circle and bounded away. He worked silently, nose to the ground, trotting along an invisible trail.

Left. Right. Toward the back of the house and then away.

No bark of alert. No sprint back to indicate that someone was nearby. They'd been doing this together for years, and Justin knew his dog well enough to know that the Malinois sensed no danger.

His skin crawled, anyway.

He had a feeling about this. One he couldn't shake. Boyd might not be there now, but Justin's gut said he had been.

"What do you think?" Gretchen asked quietly.

"Whoever was here is gone," Justin responded, watching as Quinn ran back to the door. He nudged it with his nose, and it swung open, creaking on old hinges.

Quinn didn't enter. He just glanced back over his shoulder to see if Justin was following.

"Front!" Justin called, and Quinn sprinted back, stopping short directly in front of him and sitting there, tongue lolling, a happy smile on his face.

"Why would Boyd enter an empty house and then leave?" Gretchen asked, her gaze focused on the open door. "He's been keeping pretty well hidden. He obviously has safe places to go to ground."

"I was wondering the same thing," Justin admitted, walking to the door and shining his flashlight on the opening. He was looking for signs of a booby trap, evidence that Boyd had left something dangerous behind. He wasn't the kind of criminal who did things without careful planning and thought. He was smart, meticulous and, thus far, one step ahead of Justin and the base police.

"A booby trap, maybe?" Gretchen suggested what he was thinking. "Or a bomb?" She crouched, peering into the dark house.

Justin continued his search of the door. From what he could see, there was no trip wire and no evidence that the door had been booby-trapped.

"If he was here, he had an agenda, and it wasn't just finding a place to hang out for a couple of hours," he responded. "I'll call in our explosive detecting team. Nick Donovan and his K-9, Annie, can check things out before we go in and look around."

Quinn snuffled the ground nearby, then made a circuit of the yard. It wasn't large, but someone had planted several trees. At one point, there had been a garden. Now old vines and dead plants filled a weed-choked patch of cleared land. An old swing set sat near the edge of the property. Beyond that, thick woods spilled out into deep forests. It would have been easy for Boyd to reach the house without being seen. The fact that he was on base, stalking victims again, infuriated and worried Justin.

His phone buzzed, and he pulled it out, expecting to see a text from someone at headquarters. The entire Security Forces was on high alert, ready and anxious to face off with Sullivan.

Instead, he saw Portia's number. Read the text. Felt the blood drain from his head.

I've got your daughter. Three guesses where I'm hiding her.

"What's wrong?" Gretchen asked, leaning in close and eyeing the message on his phone.

"It was a setup! He has Portia," he said.

"Boyd? How? Didn't you hire twenty-four-hour protection for her?" Gretchen asked, but Justin was already running back to the SUV, Quinn loping beside him.

He had to get back to the house.

He had to find Portia.

Nothing else mattered but keeping his daughter safe.

* * *

There weren't a lot of things Gretchen was afraid of. Snakes, mice, spiders, the dark. She could face any of those things without blinking an eye or breaking a sweat. She knew how to take down a man twice her size, how to disarm an adversary and how to keep her cool in just about any situation. Being raised in a military family with four older brothers had made her tough, strong and—she hoped—resilient.

So, fear? It wasn't something she was all that familiar with.

Right now, though, she was afraid.

Portia was a kid. Sixteen years old. At that strange age where childishness and maturity seemed to converge into a mess of impulsivity. This was the age where kids experimented with drinking, smoking, drugs.

Portia had taken another route.

And it had turned out to be an extremely dangerous one.

Blogging about Boyd Sullivan anonymously and thinking she wouldn't get found out had put her in the crosshairs of a very deliberate and cold-blooded killer.

One who wouldn't hesitate to kill again. If Boyd really had her, if he wasn't just playing a sick game, Portia was in serious danger.

"Are you sure he has her?" Gretchen asked, hoping against hope that Justin wasn't.

But she knew him.

She'd worked with him for months, and she'd never seen him panic. Until now.

"He texted from her cell phone," he responded as he secured Quinn and jumped into the driver's seat. When he gunned the engine, she let the silence fill the SUV. She knew he was heading back to his place.

She called headquarters, explaining the situation in a succinct and unemotional way. Not because she didn't feel desperate, but because she was a military police officer. She was also a woman. Two things her old-school father had never thought should go together. She'd had to prove herself as much to him as she had to any of her fellow officers—not just being good at her job, but being exceptional. Always in control. Always following protocol. Seeking justice. Capturing criminals. Pretending that she wasn't shaken by the depravity she saw.

Boyd Sullivan was beyond depraved.

He was a psychopath. If she had to choose a word to describe him—one that her fellow officers would never hear—she'd call him evil.

He had no empathy, no remorse. He was his own law. Probably his own god.

And if he had Portia…

Please, God, let her be safe, she prayed, surprised by her sudden need to reach out for divine help. It had been a long time since she'd prayed.

She hadn't given up on God.

She hadn't stopped having faith.

Not during Henry's illness. Not during the hours she'd spent sitting beside him during chemo. Not while she'd been planning a wedding she'd known would never happen. Not when she'd held her fiancé's hand while his breathing became shallower. Even when she'd stood at his graveside listening to the pastor talk about hope during heartache, she'd trusted in God's plan.

She'd believed in His goodness.

She still did, but something in her had broken when Henry died. Four years later, and she wasn't sure if it would ever be fixed.

Tires squealed as Justin took a turn too quickly, and she eyed the speedometer. They were going too fast for the area and for the vehicle. She understood Justin's desire to get back to his house quickly, but if he didn't slow down, they might not get there at all.

"Getting into an accident won't help Portia," she said calmly.

"I'm aware of that," he muttered.

"So, how about you ease off the accelerator, or pull over and let me drive?"

"We don't have time to pull over." But he eased off the gas and took the next turn more slowly. "I should never have left her alone."

"She wasn't alone," she reminded him. "You had twenty-four-hour protection for her."

"Which failed."

"Have you heard from her bodyguard?"

"No, and I'm not foolish enough to think Boyd somehow slipped under the radar, grabbed Portia and slipped out without being noticed."

"So, you think the bodyguard has been…?" She didn't finish the question. They'd turned onto Justin's street, and she could see his house. The windows were dark, the front door closed. Everything looked locked up tight and secure.

"It looks quiet," she commented as he pulled into the driveway.

"When it comes to Boyd Sullivan, that doesn't mean anything." He braked hard, threw the car into Park and jumped out, opening the back hatch and freeing Quinn.

No discussion. No plan. This wasn't the way Gretchen operated. She liked to be methodical and organized in her approach to the job. In a situation like this—one where a serial killer could be lurking nearby—that was especially imperative.

She knew Justin felt the same.

She'd worked with him for several months, observing the way he led the Security Forces, how he approached dangerous situations, how he and his K-9 partner worked together and the way he interacted with his subordinates. He seemed to have unlimited energy and a passion for justice that was admirable.

But right now, he was running straight into danger without thinking the situation through.

She had two choices: sit in the car and wait for him to return, or run after him.

She opted for the second. She couldn't let a comrade face danger alone.

She sprinted after him, snagging his arm and yanking him to a stop. He was taller and heavier, packed with muscles he worked hard for. But she had decades of experience dealing with four older brothers who were also taller and more muscular than she was.

"Hold on!" she whispered, keeping her voice low. "We need to call for backup."

"Go ahead." He yanked away and headed around the side of the house.

"Captain, this is what Sullivan wants—you panicked and not thinking."

"I don't care what he wants. I care about Portia, and I need to see if he left anything behind. Any hint of where he took her."

"This could be a trap," she cautioned, following him into the backyard, the hair on her nape standing on end. She didn't think Boyd Sullivan would hang around waiting for Justin's return, but she couldn't guarantee that he wouldn't. He was a psychopath, extremely intelligent and determined to seek revenge for perceived wrongs that had been committed against him. Based on the file of police reports she'd read and the crimes he'd committed since escaping prison, Gretchen knew he was capable of anything.

"It's not a trap, but if you're concerned, go back to the vehicle."

"Justin, you need to slow down and think things through." She tried using his first name, speaking to him the way she did when they were off duty. He glanced in her direction, but didn't slow down. Quinn was just ahead, snuffling the ground, his ears back and his tail low.

The dog looked tense, and that worried Gretchen.

Quinn was good at finding people. She'd

been with him and Justin when they'd tracked down a kid who'd vandalized the school. She'd also been with them when Quinn tracked a guy who'd beaten his wife black-and-blue and then fled the house. She'd observed the dog several times, and she knew the posture he was displaying indicated someone's presence.

He barked and took off, running to the edge of the property, Justin on his heels. She was close behind, staying just far enough back to give them space to do their work.

They pushed through the thick foliage that surrounded the property. Gretchen followed, twigs catching at her short dark hair and scratching her face.

When Justin stopped short, she nearly slammed into his back, her hands coming up automatically, grabbing his shoulders to catch her balance.

"What—" she began.

"Quinn found the bodyguard," Justin said, crouching and giving her a clear view of what lay in the bushes in front of him. A man sprawled on the ground. She pulled her Maglite and turned it on, wincing as she saw blood trickling from the back of his head.

"Gunshot wound?" she asked, crouching beside Justin as he checked for a pulse.

"Yes. Just one to the head."

"Pulse?"

"No."

She eyed the fallen man as Justin radioed for backup and medics. The bodyguard had been dragged into the shrubs. She could see the trail his body had made—empty of leaves, dirt scraped up by his shoes. His jacket was hiked up, and his firearm was visible. Still holstered.

"He didn't have time to pull his weapon," she commented as Justin straightened.

"Boyd doesn't give people time. He doesn't play by rules. He doesn't care who he hurts. Stay here until backup arrives. I'm going inside." He called for Quinn and took off, racing back the way they'd come as if he really thought she'd stay where she was.

But he wasn't the only captain on the team.

And he wasn't thinking clearly.

That was an easy way to get killed.

Especially when someone like Boyd Sullivan was around.

She ran after him, the faint sounds of sirens drifting on the velvet night air as she sprinted across the yard, up the porch stairs and into the dark house.

TWO

Quinn didn't sense danger.

Justin was as certain of that as he was of the fact that the house was empty. He could feel it—the silence, thick and unnatural. Up until Portia had come to live with him, Justin had lived by himself. He'd been used to returning to a house that was empty and quiet. Since his daughter had arrived, things had been different, better in a way he hadn't anticipated. He'd always been a loner. He'd never thought he needed what so many of his friends had—a wife, children, family.

He'd known, of course, that if anything happened to Melanie, Portia would live with him. They'd discussed that after the death of Melanie's mother. That had been six or seven years ago, and Justin had been quick to agree that he would step in if Portia needed him. He and Melanie had been high school sweethearts.

They hadn't married, but he'd still cared about her. And he'd certainly wanted to be there for her and Portia. He'd obviously also wanted to be the custodial parent if something were to happen to Melanie. He just hadn't expected it to happen. Melanie had been young and fit, health-minded and cautious. He hadn't expected her to suddenly be gone. Portia hadn't, either. Her mother's death had been a shock. Being forced to move from Michigan to Texas had meant giving up everything she knew and loved.

For the first few months, they'd tiptoed around each other. Mostly silent. Uncertain. He'd been a little too eager to build a bridge between them. Portia had been resistant. Recently, though, they'd begun to relax around each other, and he'd begun to enjoy the music drifting from her room, the quick tap of her fingers on the laptop keyboard while he made dinner.

He couldn't remember when she'd begun sitting at the kitchen table while he cooked, but he knew he enjoyed having her there. Even when he didn't know what questions to ask or how to ask the important ones, it was nice to have a house that felt like a home. It was nice to return from work to the very real and unmistakable feeling of not being alone.

Now the house was empty, and the terror he felt at the thought of his daughter being with the Red Rose Killer stole every thought from his head. Except one: finding her.

"Portia!" he called, knowing she wouldn't answer.

Boyd had her phone. He had her.

Justin was surprised that his voice wasn't shaking, surprised that his legs were carrying him upstairs.

Quinn loped ahead of him, following a scent trail into a narrow hall that opened into three bedrooms and a bathroom. The Malinois beelined to Portia's door, scratching at it with his paw.

It opened silently, swinging inward.

"Portia?" Justin repeated, stepping inside.

The room was empty.

Just like he'd expected.

Tidy. Portia liked her things neat and organized. Just like Justin. She liked an uncluttered environment. Also, like Justin. Funny how those traits had carried genetically. Melanie had been creative and disorganized, her house filled with knickknacks and art projects.

The few times Justin had been there, he'd had the urge to declutter and organize.

Had Portia felt that way?

Had her bedroom at her mom's house been as neat and tidy as this one? He hadn't asked her. The topic had felt too fraught with emotion—a minefield he wasn't sure either of them was ready to walk through.

"I'm sorry, Justin," Gretchen said, stepping into the room behind him.

"This is my fault. I should have sent her somewhere safe."

"Nowhere would be safe. Not if Boyd wanted to get his hands on her. You know that."

He did, but that didn't make it easier to stomach.

"And the only person at fault here is Boyd," she continued, turning a slow circle, taking in all the details of the room. "There's no sign of a struggle."

"I don't think she'd have tried to fight someone who had a gun," he said, trying not to imagine the terror Portia must have felt, the fear that must have been in her eyes. She might be organized and meticulous like Justin, but she felt things deeply like her mother. She was a writer. Of journals. Of blogs. All the things she didn't say, she poured into written words and sentences and paragraphs. He didn't have to be father of the year to know that about his daughter.

"It looks like she was on her computer." Gretchen walked to the bed, moving past Justin and Quinn. He let her lead the way, because his judgment was clouded by fear. He was a good enough officer to know that, and she was a good enough one to take control of the scene.

He'd noticed the laptop, and now he noticed a note taped to it as he approached the bed. He could read it easily, the words printed in bold red ink: *Now the formerly anonymous blogger of CAFB will really have something to write about.*

"I need to find her." He called for Quinn, planning to run outside. If Quinn could find a scent trail, they might be able to follow it to Boyd's location.

"You need to slow down, Justin."

"That's an easy thing to say when it's not your daughter in the hands of a serial killer," he responded, regretting it immediately. He knew Gretchen cared deeply about the work she did and about the people she worked for. She took the job as seriously as he did, and she was as eager as he was to find and stop Boyd.

"Maybe. Probably. But we have a job to do

here, and the first step in that is figuring out where he took her."

"That's what Quinn and I are going to do."

"Find!" he commanded, and the Malinois took off, sprinting downstairs and out the door. Sirens were blaring, lights flashing on the pavement. Backup had arrived, but Justin ignored everything but his K-9 partner.

Please, God, don't let it be too late for Portia, he begged silently as he followed Quinn around the side of the house and across the backyard. The night was cool, the moon high, and he could see Quinn easily, loping toward the woods at the edge of the yard. Confident, excited, tail up, ears alert, nose dropping to the ground every few yards.

The scent trail was fresh.

They were right on the heels of Boyd and Portia. With a dog as well trained as Quinn, it would be easy to overtake them. Portia would be moving slowly. At least, he thought she would be. She'd be dragging her feet, trying to slow progress, because she was smart, and she'd know just how much she could push before Boyd reacted.

That was what Justin was telling himself.

He didn't know if it was true.

Sure, his daughter was smart—an A student who excelled at both math and English—but their bond was still tenuous and new, their knowledge of each other limited, and he really had no idea how she'd react to being kidnapped.

They reached the tree line, and Quinn trailed back toward Justin, then circled around a place where the grass seemed to have been smashed down and trampled.

"Looks like someone fell," Gretchen said, flashing her light on the spot. He hadn't expected her to stay at the house and wasn't surprised that she'd followed him. Her methods of approaching crime scenes were spot-on. She'd been an MP for six of her nearly eight years in the air force. He'd seen her military record. She was well-known for her dedication and professionalism, and he'd seen both during her time at Canyon Air Force Base.

Right now, though, he didn't want to spend time discussing the crime scene or working out the details of a plan. He wanted to find his daughter.

"You know that you can't approach this any differently than you would if we were searching for someone else's child," she added, as if she'd read his thoughts and knew exactly what he intended.

"*Kidnapped* child," he replied, but she was right. If he were searching for anyone other than Portia, he'd be meticulous as he surveyed the scene, approaching the situation logically rather than running on emotion and adrenaline.

He frowned.

Gretchen was right. He needed to slow down. He also needed to start thinking like a military police officer rather than a panicked father.

"But your comment is noted. I need to approach this like I would if it were any other case."

"Do you think she fell on purpose?" Gretchen asked, her light dancing over the crushed grass and darting toward the woods that stretched out beyond his yard.

"Maybe. Portia knows what he's capable of. She might have been trying to slow him down so that Quinn and I could catch up."

"Smart girl," she murmured, meeting his eyes. Hers were a dark rich chocolate, her features delicate and pretty. With her height and slim build, she wouldn't have been out of place on a fashion runway. A few weeks ago, a drunken airman had made the mistake of underestimating her. She'd been trying to arrest him for disorderly conduct, and he'd taken a swing at her, laughing about how he wasn't going to be taken down by a pretty little girl.

Seconds later, he'd been on the ground and in cuffs.

"Not so smart when she decided to blog about the Red Rose Killer," Justin said, "but in every other area, she seems to have a good mind. Let's hope she's slowed him down enough for us to catch them."

"He's going to be expecting us to use Quinn. You know that, right? He'll be watching, making sure that we're not coming up from behind."

"We don't have any other option," he said, watching as Quinn nosed the ground near an old spruce.

"What did he say in his text?" she asked.

"That he had her, and he'd give me three guesses as to where they were."

"So, he thinks you'll know where he's taking her."

"He likes to play games. You know that, Gretchen."

"You two have a history together. I know he was here before he was dishonorably discharged. Did you have any run-ins with him?

Maybe something happened in a particular location that stuck out in his mind?"

"We had plenty of run-ins. I was beginning as an MP. He was a cocky, insubordinate bully."

"You had a high opinion of him even then, huh?"

"I don't have time for a trip down memory lane."

"You don't have time not to take the trip. He said he'd give you three guesses. He must think you'll be able to find him. It's what he wants, right? Not Portia. You."

She was right. Again.

"Right. We had a few run-ins. He was in a couple of fistfights with weaker recruits, and I broke things up. I caught him drinking once when he should have been in the barracks, and I wrote him up for that. I'm sure he can remember more incidents than that. He's proven his memory and his ability to hold a grudge."

"Is there any particular incident that stands out? Maybe one that got him into more trouble than any other. Or had the potential to."

There was. He hadn't thought about it in years, but his last run-in with Boyd had led to an investigation into his conduct. Eventually, his commanding officer had filed a complaint of insubordination because of Boyd's attitude and inability to take orders. That had led to his dishonorable discharge, but Boyd had always blamed Justin.

"Yes," he responded. "I caught him torturing a puppy once. He had free time on a weekend. I happened to be off duty and was hiking in the woods on base. I heard something yowling, and I followed the sound, thinking that maybe a fox or coyote had gotten itself into trouble. There's a cabin about a mile from here. Hidden in the woods."

"I've been there," she said. He wasn't surprised. The cabin had been on the property before the base existed. A hunting cabin or a rustic home built in the early 1900s, it had been left standing by the air force and was sometimes used as a hiding place during K-9 scent training.

"The sound was coming from there. I wasn't trying to be quiet when I approached. I figured if there was an animal that wanted to get out before I arrived, I'd rather have it gone. Boyd walked out the door as I was crossing the clearing. He had a knife in a sheath on his thigh, and for a couple of seconds, I thought he might pull it on me. I asked what was going on, and he said he'd found a dog trapped in the chimney and freed it. He walked away. I went in the cabin, and found the German shepherd puppy. He was really young. Maybe nine or ten weeks old."

"Was it dead?"

"No. His fur was singed, though. Like someone had been holding a match to it. I had no idea how he'd gotten there, and I still don't. I brought him to the base vet and found out the poor guy had a broken hind leg and a couple of cracked ribs. He survived, and I fostered him until he was able to go into our working dogs training program. Scout is now one of the best German shepherds on the team, one of the four superstar K-9s. Or he was until Boyd released the dogs."

"Scout is one of the three still missing?"

"Unfortunately, yes."

"I'm assuming you turned Boyd in to your commanding officer after you found Scout?"

"Yes. He said nothing could be done without proof. I wasn't satisfied with that. A guy who'd hurt an animal is just as likely to hurt a human being. I went to Boyd's commander and told him the story. Boyd already had a history of insubordination. A couple of days later, he was dishonorably discharged."

"And he blames you."

"He blames everyone but himself," he responded, his mind on that day and the cabin, his thoughts suddenly clear. "The cabin has to be where he took her."

"That makes sense. So, how are we going to approach it? He's probably waiting to ambush you. Based on his history, I doubt he's going to give you a chance to strike. He'll be expecting Quinn to move in first—an early-warning system for him. Maybe we hold Quinn back?"

"*We* aren't going to do anything. You're going to stay here and inform backup."

"Backup is on the way and radios work well. I'll call in the information, but I think you know I'm not standing down."

He did, but he'd had to try. He'd lost a partner before. That was a loss he never wanted to experience again.

He glanced back the way they'd come and could see lights dancing along the ground as Security Forces officers headed toward the edge of the property. He could wait for them, but had to get to the cabin. He knew how long it would take to get there.

He knew that Portia was waiting for him to arrive. That she was scared and in danger.

That was all he could think about. All he could focus on.

He shrugged his agreement, hooked Quinn to his leash and stepped into the forest.

She was moving slowly, following Justin and Quinn as they wound their way into the woods. What Gretchen wanted to do was run. She'd been to the cabin a few times, and she had an excellent sense of direction. Probably thanks to her parents' deep love for adventure, she'd learned young how to find her way through the wilderness. The moon was high, the stars bright. She could navigate using the sky, and she could move a lot more quickly while she was doing it.

Justin seemed content to walk at a steady reasonable pace, Quinn on the leash beside him.

"We're not that far from the cabin, are we?" she asked quietly, searching the moonlit forest for landmarks.

"Less than two miles."

"So it wouldn't have been difficult for Boyd to get Portia there."

"Not difficult, but not easy, either. Not if Portia was trying to slow him down. This forest can be hard to navigate during the day. At night, it's more challenging."

"I'm sure he had the route timed and took into consideration his kidnapping vi—Portia."

"Victim. You can call her what she is. Let's just make sure she stays a kidnapping victim and nothing more."

Quinn pranced a few feet ahead, his tail and ears up, his nose to the ground.

"It looks like Quinn is on Sullivan's trail," she commented.

Justin nodded. "His or Portia's."

"What's the plan for when we reach the cabin?"

"We keep Portia and ourselves alive and apprehend Sullivan."

"I was hoping for a few more details."

"We'll assess things when we get there."

She would prefer to assess things now.

She liked to know what she was going into and how she was going to get out of it. Not just in work. In life.

She'd enjoyed working with Justin these past few months because he was the same. Careful. Methodical.

"I think we'd be better off stopping for a couple of minutes and coming up with a solid plan about how we're going to approach the cabin. Boyd Sullivan is—"

"I know what he is." He stopped suddenly,

and she realized that Quinn had stopped, too. The dog was just a few feet ahead, stiff and alert, staring through thick undergrowth.

"What does he see?" she whispered.

"The cabin."

"Where?" She moved closer, stepping up beside Justin. He was taller than her by several inches. That had surprised her when she'd met him. She was used to being eye to eye with her male coworkers.

He pointed but didn't speak, his arm brushing hers, the fabric of his uniform rasping quietly. The forest had gone silent except for the distant sounds of backup moving through the woods. She'd spent enough time outside at night to know what she should be hearing. Animals scurrying through the trees. Deer picking their way through the forest. The rustle and sigh of leaves as predatory birds searched for prey.

Moonlight filtered through the thick tree canopy, bathing the world in its green-gray glow. Tall evergreens and shorter, thicker oaks stood as silent sentinels, guarding a clearing that Gretchen could just see through the foliage.

The cabin was there. Four walls. A thatched roof. Empty holes where windows and doors had once been. She couldn't see the details—just the right angles of the old exterior walls—but she'd explored the woods and seen the cabin. She'd also been on training exercises with K-9 puppies. She could picture the building—its size and shape and access points for the interior. It would be easy to get inside, but not as easy to do so undetected.

"This way," Justin said, his words more breath than sound.

He led the way through the undergrowth, bypassing the thickest sections. Quinn moved silently in front of them, disappearing for a few seconds, then reappearing. He didn't need to be commanded to remain quiet. He'd been trained well. He knew his job and seemed to have endless enthusiasm for it.

He stopped at the edge of an overgrown clearing, moonlight glinting in his tan fur, scruff raised, ears forward and down. He sensed danger, and he was letting Justin know it.

Gretchen tensed, eyeing the clearing and the old cabin that sat in the center of it. She could see it plainly now. That meant anyone inside could possibly see them.

Light danced across a window opening, disappearing as quickly as it appeared.

"He's there," Justin muttered as if it had ever been a question in either of their minds.

She grabbed his arm, pulling him back a few steps. "You aren't planning to step out into that clearing, are you? Because if we can see the cabin, anyone in it can see us."

"My daughter is in there," he responded.

That didn't answer the question.

It didn't make her feel any better about the situation.

"I'm aware of that," she replied, keeping a tight grip on his arm. "If he takes you out before you reach the cabin, what's going to happen to Portia?"

"If he takes me out, it'll ruin the game. Sullivan isn't about that. He wants to see my face and know that he's got me where he wants me—scared and helpless."

"You're not either of those things."

"I'm not *one* of those things, but let him think what he wants. It'll keep me alive until I can free Portia."

"Until? What about after?" she whispered, but he pulled away, breaking her grip easily.

"Stay here and stay hidden. He's got nothing to lose by taking you out."

He stepped into the clearing with Quinn, and she almost followed.

But Justin was right.

Sullivan had no grudge against her, no game he wanted to play with her. He had no reason to want to watch her suffer. If she stepped out into the clearing, the first bullet he fired would be at her.

He'd save the next for Quinn. Then Portia.

Finally, after he took everything Justin cared about, he'd kill him.

She slipped back into the woods, skirting around the clearing, listening to the eerie silence and the wild beat of her heart. She wasn't afraid for herself. She was terrified for Justin and for Portia. Boyd Sullivan had come to Canyon Air Force Base to seek vengeance for perceived wrongs, and Justin was probably at the top of the list of people he wanted to destroy. The fact that Portia was in danger seemed to be clouding Justin's judgment, and clouded judgment could easily get a law enforcement officer killed. Especially in a situation like this.

She stepped out of the woods near the back of the cabin and moved silently across the clearing. She could hear Justin moving on the other side of the building, his footsteps crunching on dead leaves and twigs. He wasn't trying to be quiet. He probably figured there was no reason. Boyd knew he was coming but had no idea Gretchen was there, too.

She'd use that to her advantage.

She crept close to the light-colored log walls of the cabin. There'd been two windows cut into the facade, and she approached one, freezing as she saw the flashlight beam sweep across one of the openings and then the other.

"I know you're out there," a man called in a singsong voice that made her blood run cold.

For a moment, she thought she'd been seen, that somehow Boyd had realized Justin wasn't alone.

She dropped to her stomach, her left side pressed close to the cabin, her right arm free to pull her service weapon.

"Blackwood!" the man continued. "Move a little faster, or your little girl is going to die."

"Dad! No!" Portia called, her voice wobbly with tears. "He's going to shoot you!"

"Shut up!" Boyd yelled in response, the quick hard crack of flesh against flesh ringing through the night.

For a moment, there was nothing but silence, and then the soft pad of feet on the ground. Justin was moving again, and Gretchen wasn't going to let him go into the situation alone. She crept toward the window, staying low to the ground as she moved toward the old cabin, the sound of Portia's terror still ringing in her ears.

THREE

Justin had spent most of his adult life keeping his anger in check. His father had been a raging alcoholic with a mean and violent temper. The day Justin had left home for basic training, he'd vowed he'd be a better man. He liked to think he had been. He'd avoided the trap of alcohol and anger. He'd treated people with empathy and kindness. Even on the job, even with known criminals, he'd focused on justice rather than revenge.

Right now, though, he wanted to drag Boyd from the cabin and make him pay for putting his hands on Portia.

His muscles were tight with anger and tension, his movement stiff as he approached a gaping hole that had once been a door.

"Leave the dog outside, Blackwood," Boyd commanded.

Boyd thought he had the upper hand, and he

seemed happy to let the game play out for a while longer. That was fine by Justin. He could hear Security Forces officers moving through the woods. It wouldn't be long before the cabin was surrounded.

"Down," he commanded, and Quinn dropped to his belly, growling deep in his throat as he eyed the doorway.

"Good boy," Boyd said, laughing coldly. "You. Not the dog, Blackwood."

If he wanted to get a rise out of Justin, he was going to be disappointed. Having his judgment clouded by emotion wasn't going to help him get Portia out of this situation alive. That was his goal, his mission and his focus. Boyd's games were incidental.

"Nothing to say to that?" Boyd taunted. "I guess you're not as big a man as you pretended to be when I was in basic training."

"Let Portia go," Justin responded, ignoring the taunt. "She's a child."

"She's a teenager. One who likes to post junk on the internet she knows nothing about."

"I'm sorry," Portia said. "I shouldn't have written any of those things about you, Mr. Sullivan."

"Do you think an apology is going to save your dad?" Boyd replied.

"I just—"

"It's not!" Boyd snapped. "Me and your dad go way back, and there's nothing good between us."

"I'm sorry," Portia repeated, and Justin wondered if she was trying to keep Boyd's focus away from him.

"Shut up! Blackwood, get in here!"

Justin stepped across the threshold and into the cabin's main room. Decades ago, the place may have been someone's home. Now it was nothing more than a carcass made of old logs. In addition to the missing windows, the door and part of the roof were missing. Moonlight illuminated the interior, and he could see Portia sitting on the ground a few feet away. Her face was pale, her hair falling across her cheeks. She looked more like Melanie than she did Justin—her build delicate, her cheekbones high.

Boyd stood beside her, tall and lean, his eyes gleaming with dark amusement. He had a gun in his right hand and a flashlight jutting from his jacket pocket. If he were worried about being captured, he wasn't showing it.

"Well, well," he said. "Here we are. Finally face-to-face. After all these years, you probably thought you were going to get away with what you did to me."

"I don't recall doing anything," Justin responded, taking a step in Portia's direction.

"Don't," Boyd said, his voice cold with rage. "I would hate to kill your daughter before the party even got started."

"This isn't the kind of party I like," Portia said, and Boyd's gaze cut to her.

"No one asked you, Ms. Bigmouthed Blogger."

"If that's the best insult you can come up with—"

"That's enough, Portia." Justin cut in before she could say more. Goading Boyd would only anger him, and right now, Justin wanted things to stay calm.

"Good call, Blackwood. Now, how about we all take a little walk?" He grabbed Portia's arm and dragged her to her feet.

To her credit, she didn't resist, and she didn't cry out.

She looked terrified, though—her eyes wide and filled with fear.

"It's going to be okay, Portia," Justin said.

Boyd laughed. "That depends on what side of the gun you're standing on. Speaking of which..." He lifted his gun and pressed it to

Portia's temple. "What's it feel like to come face-to-face with the guy you called inept, blogger-girl? Do you still think I'm stupid?"

Justin's heart stopped.

He stared into Portia's eyes, trying to convey a sense of control and comfort that he didn't feel. Trying to discourage her from giving a flip teenage response.

Boyd could and would pull the trigger.

He'd done it before.

"Let her go, Boyd," Justin said, keeping his voice calm. He didn't want to escalate things.

"You don't call the shots anymore, Blackwood." Boyd chuckled, the pistol easing away from Portia's temple but still aimed at her. "Get it? Call the shots? You're not laughing. I guess you're as boring and uptight as ever. Man, it's been a long time, hasn't it?"

"Not long enough."

"I disagree. I'd have been happy to take you out months ago. I should have thought about her before now." He jabbed the gun closer to Portia. "Seems you'll do anything to keep your kid alive."

"I will," Justin agreed, and Portia shook her head.

"Dad—"

"This is a grown-up conversation, blogger-girl," Boyd growled. "You keep your mouth shut. Where's the dog, Blackwood? We're leaving, and I don't want him coming at me when we step outside."

"He won't bother you." Not until Justin called him. Once he did, Quinn would be on Boyd like a missile—quick and deadly accurate.

"He'd better not. Your daughter's life depends on it. She sure is a pretty little thing." He flicked Portia's hair with the muzzle of his pistol, chuckling when she flinched.

"She's a kid. A little girl," Justin said, his voice gritty with banked anger.

"A teenager who knows her way around a computer. Not a kid. I don't kill kids," Boyd spit. "But I do kill annoyances, and you're both that."

"She wrote a few anonymous blog posts. What's that matter to a guy like you?"

"It matters. It all matters." The gun swung toward Justin and then back in Portia's direction. "You did this, Blackwood. You did all of it. I might have pulled the trigger and fired at those people, but you called the shots. Do you regret it? Do you have any remorse?"

"Maybe if you tell me what I did—"

"You know what you did! I would have done

just fine in basic training. I would have excelled. I would have been top of the class. Except for you."

"I don't like bullies, Boyd. I don't let them prey on people weaker than they are. I don't allow them to hurt defenseless animals."

"Everyone there was weaker. That wasn't my fault. I was taking my rightful place as the leader of the pack. You work with dogs. You should understand how that goes. And as for that puppy, I didn't do anything but save his life, and look at him now—one of the top dogs on your team." The pistol was slipping again, the muzzle dropping.

Portia noticed. She met Justin's eyes, shaking her head slightly. He knew the message she was sending him silently. She didn't want him to act, didn't want him to try to disarm Boyd, but that was the only way to save her.

"He was. Now he's missing. Thanks to you."

"Right. Consequences stink, don't they?" He grinned.

"I guess you'd know about that more than I would. You were insubordinate in basic training, and you got a dishonorable discharge. You went home and killed five people, and then got sent to federal prison. You escaped and started killing again, and you're going to be thrown in prison again," Justin said, purposely riling him up, getting him angry, trying to keep him from thinking, from noticing that Justin was edging nearer.

A few more steps, and he'd be close enough to lunge for the weapon.

"I'm not going back to prison, Blackwood," Boyd said coldly. "Men like me never do."

"Like you? You think you're too smart to get caught?" he asked, taking another step forward. "You made a mistake tonight. You should have come after me and left Portia alone."

"I don't make mistakes!" he screamed. The gun moved, and for a split second, Justin thought he'd won, that Boyd would release his hold on Portia and go after him.

But as quickly as Boyd's anger appeared, it was gone.

"Good try, Blackwood," he said. "But I know what you're trying to do."

"Maybe you could explain it to me?"

"Put your gun on the ground. Now. And do it slowly. You so much as make me think you're taking aim, and I kill your daughter."

Justin played along, taking his handgun from its holster and setting it on the floor.

Something moved in the window behind

Boyd, a flurry of shadows that coalesced into a figure climbing silently through the opening. Slim. Tall. Graceful and quick.

He had about two seconds to realize it was Gretchen.

He wanted to tell her to stop, but it was too late.

Boyd must have sensed her presence. He swung around, firing a shot almost blindly.

Justin grabbed Portia, yanking her away and thrusting her through the doorway, shouting for Quinn.

The dog was there, snarling and snapping, rushing toward Boyd, who still had his gun in hand.

"Call him off or she dies," he yelled shrilly, his firearm aimed at Gretchen.

She lay still.

Stunned or injured or afraid to move.

"Quinn, off!" Justin shouted, and the dog backed off, still growling, still snarling. Unhappy to have been called off his prize.

Justin moved toward Gretchen, freezing when Boyd dragged her to her feet and pressed the gun into her side. She was a rag doll, limp and helpless in his grip.

"Don't move," Boyd commanded. "Don't even breathe."

The world went silent.

Not a breath of sound.

And then chaos reigned again. Gretchen moved suddenly, thrusting her hand under Boyd's chin, slamming her elbow into his gut. The firearm discharged, the bullet slamming into the dirt floor.

Boyd backhanded Gretchen, propelling her toward Justin.

He caught her, lowering her to the ground and grabbing his gun at his feet. He came up and fired a shot as Boyd jumped through the window. He wanted to follow, but Gretchen was injured and Portia was standing in the doorway, her soft sobs filling the cabin. Obviously, she'd been too terrified to make a run for it. He didn't dare leave them alone. Not with Boyd on the loose.

"It's okay, Portia," he said quietly, holstering his weapon. "He's gone."

She'd been shot. That was Gretchen's first thought. Her second thought was that Boyd Sullivan was escaping. She pushed herself to her knees, surprised when someone took her arm, holding her steady as she got to her feet.

Not someone.

Justin.

He'd shrugged out of his jacket and was pressing it to her shoulder. She brushed it away. "I'm fine."

"You're bleeding a lot, Gretchen," Portia said, hovering a few steps away, her eyes wide with fear, her face pale.

"You call this bleeding?" She scoffed, offering the teen an encouraging smile. "You should have seen me when I fell out of the tree my brothers dared me to climb. I hit my head on the way down and bled so much they thought I was dead."

"You have brothers?" Justin asked, pulling the fabric of her jacket and shirt away so he could see the wound. The bullet had grazed her upper arm, and dark blood bubbled from the wound. She didn't feel any pain. All she felt was anger. That Boyd had struck again. That a man was dead. That a teenager had been terrorized. That a man who killed indiscriminately was escaping again.

"I have four brothers." She brushed Justin's hand away. "Stop fussing. I'm fine."

"Sure you are. If fine is having a bullet take a chunk out of your upper arm," he responded, pressing his jacket to the wound to try to stanch the bleeding.

She felt that. The pressure on the open

wound made her grimace, but she wasn't going to admit that she was in pain. She brushed his hand away again. "The bleeding has almost stopped, and Boyd needs to be captured. Take Quinn and go after him. I'll watch Portia until backup arrives."

He hesitated, and she knew he was torn. He didn't want to leave his daughter, but he knew how important it was to apprehend Boyd.

"I'll make sure Portia is okay, Justin. I promise," she assured him.

"It's not just her I'm worried about," he replied, but he'd moved to the window Boyd had escaped through. "You're pale and still bleeding. You probably need stitches."

"I can get stitches with or without you nearby."

"Dad, please don't go," Portia cut in, grabbing Justin's arm as he leaned out the window opening.

"Portia, he needs to be stopped. Tonight. Before he hurts anyone else. Gretchen will make sure you're okay—"

"I'm not worried about me," the teen protested. "I'm worried about you."

"Your dad is going to be okay, too," Gretchen said, putting a hand on Portia's shoulder and wishing she were better at this part of the job. She'd gone into military police work because she'd believed in justice, and because it had seemed like the thing to do. Her father had worked as an MP until he'd retired. All four of her brothers were military police officers, and from the time she was old enough to remember, she'd wanted to follow in their footsteps. She'd been the youngest by nine years. A surprise that had pleased her parents and her brothers. She'd been encouraged to pursue her dreams, and military life had been the only one she'd had.

Until Henry.

He'd made her want the things she'd written about in her adolescent diary—love and romance and forever. By the time she and Henry met at an on-base church, she'd already established herself as a tough no-nonsense military police officer. Tough was a necessity when you were a woman in a man's world. Showing empathy, sympathy and sorrow were not. Henry had appreciated that. He'd been Airman Second Class, back from Afghanistan and training new recruits. They'd hit it off immediately.

If things had worked out, Henry would have finished out his final year in the military and then applied to the FBI. Gretchen would have spent another four years working and then left the air force to start a family with him.

But things hadn't worked out.

And now she was in an old cabin in the middle of the woods with a teenager who needed the kind of nurturing support Gretchen hadn't had any practice with.

Portia still had Justin's arm, her eyes dark in her pale face. "Dad! Really! You can't go after him. He wants to kill you."

"Gretchen is right. I'm going to be fine. Quinn is smart and quick, and he always has my back."

"He's a dog, and he can't stop a bullet. You know Boyd Sullivan will shoot you as soon as he gets a chance."

"I'm not going to give him a chance," Justin assured her.

"That's what you think is going to happen, but you can't know for sure that you can stop him. Look what happened to Mom. She was going to work. Just like she did every Wednesday night. She should have made it home, and she didn't." Portia swiped at a tear that was sliding down her cheek, and Gretchen wanted to pull her close, tell her again that everything was going to be okay. That her father would return. That Boyd would be caught. That life would go on, and that she'd continue on with it. That, one day, she'd think of her mother, and she'd be happier for the times they'd had than sad for the times they'd missed.

But those were big concepts. Difficult ones.

Gretchen was nearly thirty, and she struggled to accept her loss. Even four years after his death, she missed Henry and what they'd planned together.

Portia was a kid.

One who'd lost her mother. It wasn't surprising that she was terrified of losing her father.

"I wish I could stay here with you," Justin said, pulling Portia in for a hug.

She went stiff, her arms down at her sides.

"If you really wished it, you'd stay," she muttered.

"I have a job to do, Portia. And if I don't do it, you'll never be safe." He stepped back, his voice as stiff as Portia's hug had been.

"If you die it's going to be my fault. Just like—" She stopped and stepped back, her expression tight and guarded.

"Just like what?" he asked.

"Nothing." She was lying. Gretchen didn't know much about teenagers, but she knew a lie when she heard one.

Justin hesitated, staring into his daughter's eyes as if he could find the secret she was keeping.

Outside, a dog barked and dry leaves crackled. Lights bounced across the clearing. Help had arrived. Finally.

"I need to go," Justin said. "We'll discuss how none of this is your fault later. Stay with Gretchen. Do whatever she tells you without arguing."

"But—"

"It really is going to be okay, Portia," he said, and then he issued a command to Quinn, waited for the Malinois to bound through the window and follow him. He had to find Boyd. He had to stop him.

Tonight.

Before he had the chance to hurt anyone else.

FOUR

He didn't want to leave.

That was a problem that Justin hadn't anticipated.

He'd spent his military career as a bachelor. He'd never worried about returning home, and he'd never thought about what would happen to Portia if something had happened to him.

He'd known that she'd be okay. Melanie had been a wonderful, caring mother. He had never realized how much peace of mind that had given him. Until now.

He followed Quinn across the clearing, nearly running to keep up. The Malinois was focused and intent. He didn't seem to notice the men and women in military uniform who were swarming out of the trees. Every member of the base Security Forces wanted Boyd Sullivan caught, and they were desperate to cut off his escape.

Justin wanted to believe that would be enough, but they'd been in this position before—so close to Sullivan that his capture had seemed inevitable. Every time, he slipped through their fingers.

And now he'd gone after Portia.

Justin had been anticipating that. He'd tried to keep her safe, but even an armed bodyguard hadn't been enough.

He frowned, pushing through thick undergrowth, his heart heavy with the knowledge that another person had died. Another life lost, and Sullivan was still free.

"Captain!" a woman called.

He glanced over his shoulder and saw Ava Esposito jogging toward him, her yellow lab, Roscoe, on a leash beside her.

"Airman Esposito, what are you doing out here?" he asked. Ava was a K-9 handler with Search and Rescue who'd had a personal run-in with Sullivan while she'd been searching for a missing child.

"I heard about your daughter. I thought Roscoe might be able to help find her."

"She's been located."

"I heard that, too. Since I'm here, I thought we'd lend a hand in the search for Sullivan."

She tucked a strand of hair behind her ear and gestured toward Quinn. “He’s got the scent?”

“Yes.”

“How much of a head start does Sullivan have?”

“A few minutes.” He ducked under a low-hanging branch, his attention on Quinn again. Justin had worked with other dogs, but he’d never worked with one that had as much enthusiasm for the job. Quinn’s tail was wagging, his head down as he made a circuit around a large tree. This was a game to him. Boyd Sullivan was the prize. He was eager and anxious to find him.

“A few minutes is a long time in Boyd Sullivan’s world,” Ava murmured.

“Unfortunately, that’s true.”

Quinn’s head popped up, his ears twitching.

“Find!” Justin commanded, and Quinn took off, racing through the woods.

Justin raced after him, sprinting across a dry creek bed and up a steep ravine. He knew Ava was behind him, her K-9 still on his leash. Roscoe was trained in search and rescue, and he had the sweet temperament of his breed.

Quinn’s training was in apprehension.

He knew how to take down the enemy, and

he'd done it dozens of times. God willing, he'd do it tonight.

Please, Lord, Justin prayed silently, *help us stop him.*

He wanted a clear sign that God had heard, that He was ready and willing to step in and stop the carnage that Sullivan had been causing. He wanted to listen and hear some internal voice telling him that God was there, that He was working everything out for His good.

All he heard was his panting breath and heavy footfalls as his boots slapped against dead leaves.

Where are You? he wanted to ask.

Where have You been?

Years ago, he'd prayed just as desperately when his partner had been shot while they'd been responding to a domestic violence call. Justin had been a rookie military police officer. He'd been assigned to work with Corbin Williams—a twenty-year veteran of the Security Forces. They'd been partners for four years, and in that time, they'd become good friends. Corbin had included Justin in family events, invited him to church, helped him mature as a Christian.

And then they'd gone on the call that had changed everything.

One shot fired by a drunken airman and Corbin had fallen. The bullet had punctured his lung and lodged in his liver. He'd lived long enough to see his wife and his kids at the hospital. During surgery to remove the bullet and repair the damage, his heart had stopped.

Justin's desperate prayers hadn't saved him.

His prayers hadn't eased the heartache of Corbin's family.

If Corbin had been around, he'd have told Justin that God works even the difficult times into good things.

And maybe he'd have been right.

Justin had gone into K-9 work because he hadn't wanted to lose another partner. Corbin had been his first and last human partner. Over the years, he and K-9 partners had stopped a lot of criminals and saved a lot of lives.

Corbin's widow, Alexis, reminded Justin of that when he visited. She lived in Houston now. The kids were grown. She had grandkids. And she never doubted that God was with her. That He loved her.

Justin tried to have that kind of faith.

More often than not, he failed.

Right now, though, he wished he could hold on to the promises that Corbin had so often quoted when they were on the job together. He wished he could access the kind of belief in God's divine plan that didn't waver. No matter the circumstances.

Instead, all he managed were quick, desperate prayers that seemed as ineffective as umbrellas during hurricanes.

Up ahead, lights gleamed through the trees. Not house lights. Streetlights.

Sullivan was running toward an escape vehicle.

The thought left Justin cold.

He'd been hoping they had him boxed in.

"He has a vehicle waiting," Ava said, echoing his thoughts.

"Radio in our location. See if we can get some manpower here. We'll want to block the road..." His voice trailed off as Quinn suddenly appeared. The Malinois ran to him, jumping up and planting his feet on Justin's chest. One quick bark, and the dog was off again.

"He's found him," Justin yelled, racing after the dog.

The trees thinned out and the forest opened up into a grassy field. Beyond it, he could see a brick building and an empty parking lot.

The church.

He and Portia attended every Sunday, and it

didn't surprise him that Boyd would go there. He loved instilling fear. This was a place Justin felt comfortable and at ease. Boyd wanted to change that.

Behind Justin, Ava was speaking quickly, relaying their location, calling for police presence at the church and on the streets surrounding it.

Too little too late.

Sullivan had planned this well. He'd parked far enough away to have built-in escape time. He'd parked close enough that walking had been easy.

And he'd made a stop at the empty property, broken in, turned on some lights. Stretched the Security Forces thinner by giving them another location to search.

"I want this guy. Tonight," Justin muttered as he raced across the field. He could see Quinn, moonlight glinting in his fur, his body tense as he loped through the grass.

He was heading straight toward the church, not sniffing, not searching. He'd seen his prize, and he was leading Justin to it.

A car engine revved as Quinn reached the parking lot, and Justin's pulse jumped, his hair standing on end.

Quinn was heading into the fray, ready to

take Sullivan down. But a car was a deadly weapon, and Justin wasn't willing to lose another partner.

"Front!" he yelled, and Quinn's ears twitched, his powerful body jerking to a stop.

He swung around, running back toward Justin as a vehicle raced around the side of the building and sped straight toward them.

Justin pulled his firearm, aiming for the car's windshield. His first shot shattered the glass.

The car spun to the left, the engine revving again as Sullivan fled. Of course he wouldn't stand his ground. He was a coward. Just like most bullies.

Justin fired another shot, taking out a back tire. The car fishtailed but kept going, crippled but still functioning. Hopefully not for long.

He radioed in a description of the vehicle, offering a partial plate number and asking that gate security officers be made aware of the situation. He doubted Sullivan would attempt to drive off base, but he wanted to be prepared if it happened.

Quinn whined, still sitting in front of Justin, staring into his face as if he had some secret message to convey.

"What is it, boy?" Justin asked.

Quinn jumped up, front paws on Justin's chest for a second before he sat again.

"That's his indication," Ava commented. Not a question, but Justin nodded. Sullivan was gone, but Quinn had something else he wanted to go after.

"Go get it, Quinn," he commanded.

The dog bounded away, running into the parking lot, away from the pebbly pieces of glass that glinted in the moonlight. He reached the church, rounded a corner and disappeared from sight.

"Do you think we should call in the bomb unit to check the church?" Ava asked. "I wouldn't put it past Sullivan to use something like that as a distraction."

"I don't think he planned on being followed back here, so I think we're in the clear."

"He's been excelling at staying a step ahead of us, Captain," she reminded him. "Anything is possible."

"I agree, but he had no reason to believe I'd be able to follow him here. He planned to kill me in the woods, and he isn't used to failing. He'd have assumed he was going to get the outcome he was looking for."

"He is cocky and arrogant, so you could be right. That will work out well for us. Arrogant, cocky people tend to make mistakes."

"And mistakes get criminals caught."

They rounded the corner of the building to find Quinn standing beneath a streetlight. Ears back, muzzle down, he stared at something that lay on the ground.

"Off!" Justin commanded. Quinn was well trained. He wouldn't touch the item. He wouldn't eat it.

But Sullivan was familiar with the K-9 team. He'd been observing it for months. He had to know how tight the bond was between handler and K-9 partner. Justin wouldn't put it past him to try to poison the dogs. He certainly hadn't cared about releasing the well-trained dogs from their kennels.

"Heel," he said as Quinn reached his side.

The dog did as he was commanded, stepping into heel and matching his pace with Justin's.

Justin motioned for Ava to stay back, then approached the streetlight. After a few steps, he could see the item clearly. *Items.* A long-stemmed red rose lying on top of a piece of paper. He crouched beside it, pulling out his phone and snapping a few photos.

"What is it?" Ava asked, approaching cautiously.

"A rose."

"Sullivan's signature," she murmured. "Is that a note?"

"Yeah. It says, *'You're next.'*"

"Did he think you hadn't already figured that out? He did kidnap Portia to get to you."

"He's enjoying the game. He won't be for much longer," he responded grimly.

"Let's see if we can track the vehicle," Ava suggested. "He won't get far with a blown-out tire. Once we find the car, we should have no problem tracking him from there."

"You are Search and Rescue, Ava," Justin pointed out. Ava had been key in helping to locate many of the dogs Boyd had freed from the base kennel, and she continued to search for the ones that remained missing. A few months ago, she'd helped find a child who'd been missing from a school trip. During her search, she'd come face-to-face with Sullivan. Since then, she seemed determined to be part of the team efforts to bring in the serial killer.

"And?"

"Security Forces will handle searching for Sullivan."

"We're all part of the same team, Captain," she reminded him. "And Roscoe's got a great nose. The scent is fresh. Now is the time to go."

She was already walking toward the street, Roscoe beside her.

"He's not trained in apprehension or attack, and Sullivan won't care whether he takes out a mild-tempered Labrador or a high-energy Malinois."

She hesitated. He'd known she would.

K-9 teams were strongly bonded, and no handler would put a dog into a situation he hadn't been trained for.

"Are you taking Quinn?"

He wanted to, but three Security Forces vehicles were speeding into the lot, officers jumping out and running toward him. He could count on his MPs to do everything in their power to apprehend Sullivan, but if Sullivan slipped through their fingers, he knew where he needed to be. At the hospital.

Portia was there with Gretchen, who was injured.

The thought of either of them coming up against Boyd made his pulse race.

"I'm going to the hospital. I need to make sure Portia and Gretchen are okay," he responded, his attention on the officers who were moving toward them. Tech Sergeant Linc Colson was there, opening the back hatch of his vehicle and letting his rottweiler out.

Good.

Star was a trained attack dog. She'd be able to take Sullivan down easily. If they were able to track him down.

"Captain," Linc called, raising a hand in salute. "I hear there's been another run-in with Sullivan."

"He killed a bodyguard and kidnapped Portia."

"Does he still have her?"

"Gretchen and I managed to free her, but Sullivan slipped through our fingers. Again." He filled Linc in on what had transpired, giving a description of the car and the direction Sullivan was heading.

Hopefully it would be enough.

The Red Rose Killer needed to be brought to justice before anyone else was hurt or killed.

"We'll do everything we can to bring him in," Linc assured him. "Are you heading to the hospital?"

"Yes."

"Take my vehicle. I can catch a ride back to headquarters and grab the SUV later." He tossed keys in Justin's direction, issued a terse command to Star and jogged away.

Justin wanted to believe they'd find Sullivan. He wanted to believe tonight was the night that this months-long nightmare would end, but Sullivan had eluded them over and over again. He'd killed an airman, stolen his uniform and used it to blend in while he was on base.

He was smart, and he had no conscience, no remorse.

If he got his hands on Portia again…

Justin shook the thought away, calling to Quinn and loading him into the back of Linc's vehicle. He shut the door with a little too much force, angry with himself for allowing Sullivan to escape again. Angry with God for not ending things.

Corbin had believed that there was a reason for everything. He'd often told Justin that God's plans weren't always clear, but they were always good.

Maybe he'd been right.

Probably he had been.

But Justin could see no reason for people being murdered. He could think of no good plan that involved innocent lives being lost. He'd become a military police officer because he'd believed that justice should always prevail. He'd believed that good should always win. He'd wanted to make a difference in the world, and he supposed that he had. God had used him to help dozens of people. He'd used him to solve hundreds of crimes. Justin acknowledged that, and he was grateful for it.

But this case?

It was eating him alive, because no matter how much time was put into it, no matter how many hours were spent pursuing leads, no matter what they did to try to stop him, Boyd Sullivan remained free.

"Not for long," he promised himself as he started the SUV and pulled out of the parking lot.

God was always good.

Even in the tough times.

Henry had said that often during the years they'd been together. He'd lost his father in a car accident. He'd been diagnosed with an aggressive cancer. He'd gone through chemo and radiation and been so sick he couldn't get out of bed.

And, to him, God was still good.

Funny how Gretchen had forgotten those words, forgotten how confident Henry had been when he'd said them. He hadn't been afraid to die. He hadn't been afraid to be sick. He'd lived life to the fullest until the very end.

She remembered that.

Just like she remembered his smile and his laughter.

He'd be smiling now if he were there. Joking with her while she waited for the doctor to stitch the wound in her upper arm. He'd always been happy and confident and fun. Without him, she'd become too somber and too focused, too intent on her work.

At least, that was what her closest friends said.

That may or may not have been one of the reasons she'd agreed to take the assignment at Canyon Air Force Base. She'd been at Minot Air Force Base for several years. The community there was small and tight-knit. People knew each other well, and most of them cared a lot about the happiness of their comrades.

Over the past couple of years, Gretchen had been invited on double dates, set up on blind dates and encouraged to step out of her comfort zone by friends, coworkers and acquaintances.

Apparently, there was a timeline for grief, and she should have reached the end of hers.

And in some ways she had.

Grief had faded into quiet sadness for what she'd lost and into bittersweet joy for what she'd had. But that didn't mean she wanted another relationship. She'd tried to tell her friends that. She'd tried to explain it to coworkers, but Gretchen's single status was a constant source of discussion on base, and frankly, she'd had enough of it. When she'd been asked to take a temporary transfer and train for a leadership position at another command post, she'd jumped at the opportunity.

In the months since then, she'd missed her friends and community in Minot, but she hadn't regretted the decision to leave. Even now, sitting on an exam table, arm bandaged, waiting for the doctor to return with a suture kit, she wasn't sorry she'd come to Canyon Air Force Base. She'd learned a lot, and would continue to do so for the next four weeks. At the end of that time, she'd return to Minot and begin putting together the new K-9 unit there.

Or leave the military.

She'd almost completed eight years of active service. Her commanding officer had reminded her of that when he'd offered her the temporary transfer: *You're young. You can move up the ranks and make a name for yourself, or you can leave and start a new career.*

The choice will be yours. Either way, we'll expect you to spend the last six months of your assignment setting up our new K-9 unit and putting airmen in place who will be an asset to it.

She'd agreed, because she'd needed a change of pace, because the transfer had seemed interesting, because she was always willing to learn something new.

But she'd had no idea whether she'd return to take the post as head of the Minot K-9 Unit. If she did that, she'd be committing to another four years in the military. By the time she left, she'd be thirty-two. Which shouldn't matter. She loved being an MP, but the truth was, she'd never intended to make a lifetime career of it.

"Are you okay?" Portia asked. She'd been brought to the hospital triage room at Gretchen's insistence. Anything else had been out of the question. No separate rooms. No being interviewed by the MP who was waiting in the corridor. Gretchen planned to keep Justin's daughter within arm's reach until he arrived and could take over her protection.

"Right as rain," she responded, offering the teen a bright smile.

Portia didn't seem convinced.

She tucked a strand of blond hair behind her

ear and frowned. "This is all my fault. I should never have blogged about the Red Rose Killer."

"You shouldn't have blogged about him, but that doesn't make this your fault."

"You don't have to be nice to me, Gretchen. I know that everyone my dad works with is mad at me for what I did."

"Who gave you that idea?" she asked, looking into Portia's bright blue eyes. She was a quietly pretty girl. No makeup. No oddly colored hair. Just a sweet-looking kid with dark circles under her eyes and sorrow in her expression.

"No one. It's obvious. I was writing things that my dad discussed with the team, and I was putting everyone at risk."

"Is that what your dad said?"

"Yes, and he's right."

"You're a kid. Kids make mistakes."

"My mother always said that mistakes happen. It's what we do after we make them that defines us as people."

"Your mother was a very wise woman."

"Yes. I wish…"

"She was here?" she guessed, and Portia shrugged, her gaze dropping to the floor.

"I guess that's the way every kid who loses a parent feels."

"That doesn't make it an easy feeling to have."

Portia met her eyes again. "No. You're right. It doesn't. Do you think my dad is okay?"

"Your dad is really good at what he does."

"And I'm really good at knowing when someone doesn't answer my question. I may be a teenager, but I'm not stupid."

"I think your dad is okay," she said, because she did.

But she'd seen Sullivan's handiwork. She knew what he was capable of. If he had an opportunity to kill someone he thought had wronged him, he'd take it. And he was convinced that Justin had been a big part of his dishonorable discharge.

"For now?" Portia guessed.

"We're going to capture Boyd Sullivan, and once he's in jail, everyone will be safe."

"And until he's in jail, no one will be."

"You're a smart young woman, Portia. What are you planning to do when you graduate high school? College?"

"That wasn't a subtle change of subject," Portia muttered.

"No. It wasn't, but there's not much I can say that wouldn't be a lie, and I don't lie."

"So, you're admitting my father isn't safe?"

"I'm admitting that Boyd Sullivan is dangerous. But you knew that when you were blogging about him. You did it, anyway."

"Anonymously."

"It's very difficult to stay anonymous forever. I'm sure you knew that when you started the blog."

Portia blushed. "I know it was stupid. I said I was sorry. If I could change it, I would."

"I didn't say that to make you feel bad, Portia. I said it because you decided that the blog was more important than the risks associated with it. Your father is the same. He knows the risks of his job. Every day when he goes to work, he weighs that against the importance of what he's doing. And every day he decides that what he's doing matters enough to take the risk."

"That's a good way to put it," said a deep male voice, breaking into their quiet conversation.

Gretchen turned and glanced at the open door.

Justin was standing at the threshold, Quinn sitting calmly beside him.

"Has the search ended?" she asked, hoping that he'd say it had and that Boyd was in custody.

"No. We've still got teams on the ground,

but I wanted to see how you and Portia were doing." He crossed the room and took a seat in a chair next to Portia. "Are you okay, sweetheart?" he asked his daughter.

"I'm not the one who got shot," she responded, her gaze skittering away from Justin. She seemed intent on looking at the floor, the ceiling, the walls. Anywhere but at her father.

"A person can be physically fine and mentally struggling," he responded.

"I'm fine. Mentally and physically," she said, crossing her arms over her chest and staring at her feet. All the worry she'd had for her father, all her concern about him coming up against Sullivan, was hidden beneath a facade of teenage indifference.

Justin seemed to take it in stride.

He patted Portia's shoulder and turned his attention to Gretchen. "How about you, Captain?" he asked. "Are you okay?"

"I'll be better once the doctor gets in here and stitches me up. The sooner I can get back on Sullivan's trail, the happier I'll be," she answered, looking straight into his eyes the way she had dozens of times during their months working together.

This time shouldn't have been any different.

He was the same guy she'd met a few months

ago. The captain who'd showed her around, who'd introduced her to the other MPs, who'd welcomed her to the team. At the time, she'd been aware of his height and strength, of his confidence and his excellent communication skills. The people he worked with had seemed to respect and like him, and she'd noticed that, too.

She hadn't noticed how blue his eyes were. She hadn't paid attention to the smile lines at the corners of his mouth or the thickness of his lashes. He was a coworker, a mentor, a guy she'd know for a while and then walk away from. She'd had no interest beyond that.

But right now, she was noticing his eyes. His lashes. The faint smile lines. She was thinking about how concerned he looked and how intent. Not just focused on the job, but on her well-being.

She stood abruptly, swaying a little as the blood flowed out of her head.

"Whoa! Careful," Justin said, holding her arm while she regained her balance. "You don't want to fall and knock yourself."

"What I want is the twenty-five stitches the doctor promised me," she muttered, avoiding his eyes, because she was done noticing how striking they were in his tan face.

"You're the first person I've ever known who was eager to have a needle poked through her arm," he said as she walked to the door.

"I'm eager to get back to work." And away from him, because noticing anything aside from Justin's work ethic seemed wrong. They were coworkers who were becoming friends, but that was it. For now and forever.

"You don't really think you're going straight back to work, do you?" he asked, and she knew he was watching her. She could feel the weight of his gaze, but she didn't turn around. She didn't meet his eyes. She took the cowardly way out and stared into the hall.

"I don't see why I shouldn't. Someone has to write up tonight's report."

"I can do that. I think the best thing for you to do is take some time off. Maybe a week or two."

Surprised, she swung around, realized he'd moved closer. She was tall, but she still had to look up to meet his eyes. "You're kidding, right?"

"Why would I be?"

"This is barely an injury, Captain." She raised her arm, ignoring the fact that the gauze was stained with blood.

"It looks like one to me. I may not be your

commanding officer, but I do send him weekly reports. I'm sure he'll agree that time off is a good thing."

"I only have four weeks left on base. I still have a lot to learn, and I'm not going to do that if I'm stuck at home for half the time."

"I wasn't thinking you'd be at home." He glanced at Portia. "I've already asked my commanding officer to arrange for Portia to go to a safe house."

"No way!" Portia jumped up, her hair flying around her face, her eyes dark with anger. "I'm not going."

"You're not going to have a choice," Justin said calmly. "Sullivan wants me dead, and you're the perfect way for him to get to me. Now that he knows it, he's not going to stop going after you."

"I'm sixteen. I should have some say in what happens to me."

"You can choose how you want your hair cut and what you want to eat, but you're not going to choose whether or not to stay on base when a serial killer is after you," he responded firmly. No anger. No frustration. Just a statement of fact.

Portia looked like she wanted to argue, but Justin had turned his attention back to Gretchen.

"Since we're setting that up, I thought it would be a good place for you to stay while you're healing."

"Let me make sure I have this right," she said, finally understanding. "You want me to go to a safe house until Sullivan is caught?"

"I didn't say that."

"And you're not saying it's not the truth."

"You could have died tonight," he said quietly, glancing at Portia.

"You aren't the only one who weighs the risk and then reports to work every day, Captain. I didn't become an MP to stand down when there's danger."

"I'm not asking you to do that."

"Sure you are, and I'm not sure why. Is it because I'm a woman?" she asked, because there had been men who'd thought her gender made her weaker and less capable.

She wouldn't have expected it from Justin. She'd never seen any hints of gender bias, but it was possible he'd learned to hide it during his years in the military.

"No," he responded. Flatly. Bluntly.

"Then what is it?"

He glanced at Portia again. "Not something I want to discuss right now."

"Then how about we discuss it after you transport your daughter to the safe house?"

"We'll transport her together. We can discuss the rest later," he responded, stepping to the side as the doctor finally arrived.

Gretchen was tense now, her muscles taut, and when the doctor began stitching her, the needle hurt more than it probably would have if she'd been relaxed. She'd never minded stitches, and she'd never been overly sensitive to pain, but she felt woozy, her ears buzzing as the doctor worked.

She'd lost a lot of blood.

That was for sure, but there was no way she was taking the time off that Justin had suggested.

She wasn't hiding in a safe house, either.

She'd come to Texas to be a member of Canyon Air Force Base Security Forces. That meant keeping the men and women who worked and lived on base safe. No one would be safe as long as Sullivan was free.

She had four weeks to continue her training.

Four weeks to help Justin find the serial killer who'd made the base his hunting ground.

Four weeks to make sure that Sullivan didn't strike again.

She could only pray it would be enough

time, because she wanted to be there when Boyd was captured. She wanted to watch as he was handcuffed and led away. When she returned to Minot, she wanted to know that Justin, Portia and all the people she'd met and worked with could go on with their lives, free from the fear that had been dogging them since Sullivan escaped from prison.

FIVE

Portia wasn't happy.

Justin didn't have to know much about teenage girls to know that. She sat silently in the back seat of Linc's SUV as he drove to Security Forces HQ, her eyes closed, head back, ignoring everything and everyone.

He could see her in the rearview mirror—angry and withdrawn. He was tempted to try to explain how important she was to him, how worried he was about her. But he'd done that before, outlining the situation from his perspective in an attempt to convince her that he was more concerned than angry after he'd found out she was the anonymous blogger.

She'd listened, but he doubted she'd believed him.

They had enough history together to understand a little about each other, but not enough to have an unspoken understanding about their relationship. He was her father, but he was certain she saw him more as a stranger. He wasn't someone Portia could turn to when she was upset. He wanted to be. He'd tried to be. But trust had to be earned, and all he seemed to be earning was her contempt.

He'd had no idea being the parent of a teenager was this complicated. If he'd had, he'd have thanked Melanie more than a few times a year for being such a great mother to their daughter.

He frowned, glancing in the rearview mirror again. He owed it to Melanie, to Portia and to himself to keep reaching out, to keep trying, to keep being there. Even when Portia didn't seem to want him to be.

"I know you're upset, Portia," he began.

Her eyes flew open, and she met his gaze.

"That's an understatement," she responded, turning to look out the window.

"I'm sorry. I understand that you don't want to go to a safe house, but your well-being is my top priority. I've already tried hiring bodyguards and keeping you on base. That didn't work. Now we've got to take more drastic measures."

"*You* have to take more drastic measures," she corrected. "I have nothing to do with that decision."

"You're sixteen, Portia. There are a lot of things you don't understand."

"At sixteen, I could be legally emancipated and living on my own," she retorted, her tone a little flip and a little haughty.

He tamped down irritation, trying to get to the heart of the matter rather than the emotions of it. "Reminding you that you're sixteen and that there are a lot of things you don't understand wasn't meant to be an insult."

"I didn't take it as one," she said.

"But you did mention becoming an emancipated minor," Gretchen cut into the conversation, shifting in the front passenger seat so she was facing the teen. "Is that something you've been considering?"

"No," Portia muttered. "My best friend suggested it. She thought I could become emancipated and come back to Michigan and live with her family until I graduate."

"Addie Windsor?" Justin asked, telling himself that it didn't bother him that she'd been looking for ways to get out of living with him.

She was a kid.

She'd had friends and a school and activities back in Michigan.

When Melanie died, she hadn't just lost her mother. She'd lost everything.

"It isn't about not wanting to live with you, Dad," Portia said quickly. She might be teenager with all the attitude that went with it, but she had a heart of gold. "It's about not wanting to be away from home."

"I understand," he said, because he did. The day Portia entered kindergarten, Melanie had purchased a craftsman-style home in the little town where she and Justin had grown up. He'd helped her with the down payment, and he'd requested a few days of leave to help her move in. That was the only home Portia remembered. All her memories of her childhood, her mother, her friends were there.

"Like my room. Mom let me decorate it myself last year. She let me pick out the paint color and new bedding," Portia continued, the words spilling out quickly as if she'd been holding them in for too long and finally had to release them.

"I remember," he said. He'd sent Melanie extra money to help with the cost of redecorating. She'd texted photos of the finished room with Portia and her friends sitting on the bed, beaming at the camera. He'd had no idea when he'd opened the text and seen the photos that Melanie would be gone within the month.

"Addie and Jordan came over to spend the

night after it was done, and we made a dream board that showed what we wanted to accomplish during our last two years of high school," she said with a quiet sigh.

"A dream board?" Gretchen asked. "Did you bring it with you? I'd love to see what you and your friends came up with."

"I tossed it in the trash," Portia muttered. "Three of the things were about me and Mom going places. We had a trip to the Grand Canyon planned for my senior year. And we were going to visit five colleges this year. She was excited because—" She stopped abruptly.

"She told me you were thinking about attending Michigan State. Just like she had. She was really proud of you, Portia."

Portia didn't respond.

Which was pretty much how things always went when he mentioned Melanie.

The silence stretched out for a few moments too long, and Gretchen shifted again, her injured arm bumping Justin's shoulder. "You said there were three things that you and your mother were supposed to do together," he said. "What was the third?"

"Buy my prom dress. Mom was really excited about that. I didn't even have a boyfriend, but she said going with friends would be even more fun. She never got to go to prom, because she was pregnant with me. I guess she wanted to have the experience." Her voice broke.

"I'm sorry, honey," Gretchen said. "I know how much it hurts to lose someone you love."

"Did you lose your mom?"

"No. My fiancé. Three weeks before our wedding."

Surprised, Justin glanced her way, trying to see her expression through the dark interior of the vehicle.

"Wow," Portia said. "I'm so sorry."

"So am I," Justin added. He'd never been engaged. Except for the first few days after Melanie had discovered she was pregnant, marriage had never been on his radar. He dated, but he kept things light. Dinner. A movie. He'd made it clear to any woman he'd been out with that he didn't want more. Not because he didn't sometimes think about having someone to go home to. But because his father had been an abusive alcoholic. Justin had memories of his mother being beaten black-and-blue. She'd left when he was ten, abandoning him to his father's rage. Sometimes, he could understand that. Sometimes, he couldn't. Either way, he hadn't had good examples of love when he was growing up, and he'd had no desire to see if he'd do any better.

Until the choice had been taken from him, he hadn't wanted to be the custodial parent to his daughter. He'd been afraid of what he might do, of the things he might say. He'd worried that he'd open his mouth and speak the words his father had, that he'd tear down rather than build up. That he'd create the same unforgiving and hate-filled environment he'd grown up in.

Somehow, though, that hadn't happened.

Portia had been living with him for over a year. He'd had plenty of opportunity to lose his cool and act like a raging lunatic. He hadn't. So, maybe nurture wasn't the only thing that shaped a person. Maybe faith and commitment and compassion trumped learned behaviors.

"Yeah. It was rough," Gretchen said, her voice soft and filled with emotion. "Henry and I had a whole life planned out. No dream boards, but I could picture it all in my head."

"When did he die?" Portia asked, leaning forward, apparently eager to hear the story.

"Portia, Gretchen might not want to talk about it," he cautioned, turning onto a side street that led to Security Forces headquarters. Portia would need to be interviewed by someone other than Justin. Once she'd given her statement, she'd be transported to a safe house, according to the base commander.

"I don't mind talking about it," Gretchen said, downplaying his concern. "Henry died four years ago. A little more than that actually. If things had gone the way I'd planned, I'd be retiring in six months, and Henry and I would be starting our family." She sounded matter-of-fact, but he detected a hint of something in her voice. Longing for what she might have had. Sorrow for what she'd lost. He'd assumed she was a die-hard military officer, but maybe becoming an MP had been something to do while she waited to pursue other dreams.

He didn't ask, because Portia was hanging on to her every word, nearly hanging over the seat in her eagerness to get the story. "So, you were going to have kids and everything?"

"Sure. Just because a woman is in the military doesn't mean she doesn't want those things."

"Oh, I know that," Portia said. "I've seen plenty of female officers on base who have kids. I just thought that because you were so old and not married—"

"Portia!" Justin said. "She's not old."

Gretchen laughed. "I think that depends on

what side of twenty you're standing on. What are you, Justin? Thirty-two?"

"Thirty-four," he corrected.

"I'm twenty-eight. Portia is sixteen. I'm sure, from her perspective, we're both ancient."

"Actually, I didn't mean old," Portia explained. "What I meant was that a lot of women your age are already married and have children."

"Right. How about we change the subject?" Justin suggested, and Gretchen laughed again.

"You seem more uncomfortable than I am, and I'm the one she called old."

"Really, Gretchen," the teen said, "I didn't mean that. My mom always used to say I needed to learn to think before I spoke. I guess I haven't mastered that yet."

"That's okay. Neither have I," Gretchen responded. "But since your dad wants to change the subject, how about we talk about the safe house again?"

"What about it?" Portia asked suspiciously.

"Your father is right to be concerned for your safety, and you aren't going to be safe on base."

"I can go back to Michigan for a while. I'm sure Addie and her parents will let me stay there for a few weeks. Maybe I can even take classes at the high school. Until it's safe to come back."

There was a hopeful edge to her voice that Justin didn't miss, and if he could have agreed to the plan, he would have.

"Sullivan is extremely dangerous. He's killed innocent people. Some of his victims were people he had a vendetta against. Some were just in his way," he said. "If he followed you to Michigan—"

"Don't even say it, Dad. I'd never forgive myself if something happened to Addie or her family."

"Then you understand why I can't let you do that."

"I understand, but I still want to go home," she said so quietly he almost didn't hear.

"How about we plan a trip for winter break?" he suggested, glancing in the rearview mirror. The street was empty. No cars. No people. Nothing that would lead him to believe that Sullivan was nearby. But his skin was crawling, his nerves alive with warning.

"A trip where?" Portia asked, oblivious to the danger that might be stalking them.

"To Michigan. The management company I hired to rent out your house is doing a good job, but I'd like to a do a walk-through of the property. Just to make certain everything is being maintained."

"You'd really bring me there for Christmas?" Portia asked.

"As long as this thing with Sullivan is settled, yes. Otherwise, it might have to wait until spring break." He glanced in the rearview mirror again. This time, he thought he saw a car in the distance. Lights off. Moving slowly.

"What is it?" Gretchen asked.

"Probably nothing."

"Then why do you keep looking in the rearview mirror?"

"Just a feeling."

She turned to look out the back window, her arm brushing his again. "Is that a car?"

"I think so."

"It's moving slowly. No lights. You think it's Sullivan?"

"Is it?" Portia asked, her voice shaking. "Do you think he followed us?"

"No," Justin responded. But he wouldn't put it past Sullivan to figure out where they were headed or to try to keep them from getting there. It would be a risky move. Security Forces were already out searching for him. Sullivan had to know that, but he hated making mistakes and he hated losing.

In basic training, he'd talked big, bragging that he was the best and the brightest. The strongest. The most capable. If he hadn't been a psychopath with no regard for others, he would have done okay and had a good air force career.

But he *was* a psychopath.

When he'd made mistakes during training, it had always been someone else's fault. Justin had broken up several fights that Boyd had started because he'd believed another recruit had sabotaged him or made him look bad.

No doubt, the mistake he'd made tonight, the fact that he'd almost been captured, was Justin's fault. Or Gretchen's. Or even Portia's.

Boyd would want his revenge, and he'd want it quickly.

He wouldn't care who he had to hurt to get it.

Justin accelerated, driving above the speed limit.

The car behind him did the same.

Now there was no mistaking it. The car was tailing them. And whoever was driving it meant business.

Deadly business.

Gretchen called for backup as Justin swerved onto a busier street, and then unhooked her seat belt and crawled into the back with Portia.

"It's going to be okay," she assured the teenager, her attention on the car that was still behind them.

"Is it him?" Portia asked, levering up beside her.

Gretchen grabbed her arm, pulling her down. "Keep your head down. Let's not give him a target."

"Your head is up," Portia argued, but she'd dropped low, her forehead to her knees.

"I am being paid to get a good look at the vehicle. You are not." Only she couldn't see much. Just the outline of a car flying through the red light at the intersection they'd just passed through. "He's going to kill someone," she muttered, radioing in the location and the direction they were traveling.

This section of base offered plenty of places to hide, she noted as they sped past. Several small businesses lined the streets, all of them closed at this time of night. There were alleys and Dumpsters and doors that could easily be jimmied and opened. Fences. Delivery trucks parked beside buildings.

If she were trying to elude the police, she'd be taking cover somewhere. Whoever was in the car didn't seem to have the same idea. The driver accelerated, flying through a stop sign and speeding after them. Not gaining on them but not falling behind.

"He's still there," she said even though she was sure Justin already knew that.

"It's Boyd," he replied, taking a turn a little too quickly. The SUV squealed in protest, and Quinn whined. He was either scared or eager to be out of the vehicle and on the hunt. Based on what she'd seen during the past few months, Gretchen was confident it was the latter.

"If you slow down, I may be able to get a positive ID. I don't want to shoot until I'm certain of who I'm shooting at." She opened the window anyway, leaning out and trying to get a look at the vehicle's license plate.

The driver slowed the vehicle, bumped over the curb and rolled to a stop. The door flew open, and the driver jumped out. She saw the flash before she heard the gunshot.

One. Two shots.

She had her firearm out and was pulling the trigger, protecting Portia and Justin, keeping her focus on the shooter, as Justin took another turn.

Headquarters was just ahead, and he sped into the parking lot, pulled up to the front doors and braked hard.

"Get her into the building," he shouted, hopping out of the SUV and opening Gretchen's door.

"You aren't planning on going back there," she protested as she ran around the side of the car, gun in her right hand, left arm throbbing and nearly useless. She managed to open Portia's door, anyway, grabbing the teen's hand and nearly dragging her out.

"Yeah. I am. I want Boyd behind bars. Tonight is as good a time as any to make sure that happens." Justin opened the back of the SUV and released Quinn, giving the dog the command to find and taking off before Gretchen had the door to HQ open.

"Dad!" Portia called, yanking away.

Gretchen tucked her gun into its holster and snagged the back of Portia's shirt. "We need to get inside."

"But—" The crack of a gunshot interrupted whatever she planned to say. The bullet wasn't fired from close enough to be dangerous, but that didn't mean anything. Boyd knew his way around the base, and no doubt he was working his way near enough to shoot Justin or Portia.

"Inside. Now!" Gretchen opened the door and shoved Portia into the building. An MP was running toward them, boots pounding on the tile floor.

"Take her to a room without windows and keep her there," Gretchen ordered, and then she closed the door and ran in the direction Justin and Quinn had gone. Right at the shooter.

SIX

Quinn was on the hunt, moving quickly and without hesitation. Ears up. Stride long. Focused but not sniffing the ground. Not trying to find a scent. He knew what he was after, and he knew where to find it. The question was, would they get there before Boyd escaped? Or fired off a round that hit its target?

Justin raced after the Malinois, praying that these would be Boyd's last moments of freedom. He wanted this over. Too many people had been killed. Too many people were still in danger.

As far as he was concerned, no one on base would be safe until Boyd was behind bars.

He rounded a street corner and his heart dropped.

Three MP cars were parked at the curb, lights flashing. But there was no sign of Boyd's car, and no sign of Boyd.

Someone raced up behind him, feet pounding the ground.

Gretchen.

He knew it before he turned. Knew absolutely that she'd done what he'd commanded—made sure Portia was safely inside the building.

And then she'd done exactly what he'd hadn't wanted her to do.

She'd followed him.

"I wanted you to stay with Portia in the building," he said as she reached his side. They were still running hard, Quinn suddenly pivoting away from the MPs' vehicles.

"I belong here," Gretchen responded. Not panting. Not struggling.

She had to be in pain, though.

She'd removed the sling the doctor had given her at the hospital, and he could see blood on the gauze bandage that covered the wound. "You're bleeding again."

"How about we focus on what we're here to do?" she replied. "Do you think Quinn has his scent?"

"It's possible. We've tracked vehicles before, but it will be difficult for him to follow the trail if we get to a more heavily trafficked area." And that was where they seemed to be heading. There were a few bars and restaurants in this area, most opened late.

"Which is exactly where we're headed."

"Right."

"He's done his research."

"Boyd takes pride in his intelligence. When I knew him, he loved to throw random facts out to impress people. It wouldn't surprise me if he spent months researching military working dogs and the way they work."

"Too bad he didn't take pride in his compassion for others."

"I doubt he knows what compassion feels like. He certainly wouldn't see it as a strength."

Quinn was trotting back, nose to the ground. He'd lost the scent and was trying to pick it up again. They could continue, or they could return to headquarters. If Portia hadn't been there, Justin might have been tempted to keep working the trail and letting his K-9 try to find the scent.

But the likelihood of success was small, and he was worried about Portia.

He wanted her off base and in a safe house.

The sooner that happened, the better.

"Heel," he commanded, and Quinn loped to his side.

"Good work, buddy," Justin said, scratching the dog behind his ears and under his chin.

"He looks disappointed," Gretchen said as they turned back.

"He is. He likes to win the game, and this time he didn't."

"I get the impression that you like to win, too," she commented, folding her left arm and using her right hand to support it.

"Depends on the game. When it comes to my job? Yeah. I want to win every time. Hold on." He touched her shoulder and stopped.

"You want to keep searching for him?" she asked, her attention on the road and the few cars that were driving by.

He could have told her that Boyd had probably already abandoned the car and was running as far and as fast as he could. He might want revenge, but he also wanted his freedom. Free, he could continue to terrorize people, and the desire to do that seemed to be his driving force.

"No. We'll go after him again. After I get Portia taken care of." He unbuttoned his shirt and shrugged out of it. His kept a uniform at the office, and he'd be able to replace it when he got there.

"What are you doing?" Gretchen asked as

he fashioned the shirt into a makeshift sling, his white T-shirt nearly glowing in the streetlight. If Boyd were anywhere nearby, Justin would make an easy target.

"Here." He looped the makeshift sling around Gretchen's neck, then lifted her left arm gently and slid it into place. "See? Perfect."

"Did you learn creative uses for your shirt while you were in basic training?" she asked, her cheeks pink.

He'd never seen her blush, and he found himself studying her face—high cheekbones and delicate features, full lips and flawless skin. He'd never thought of her as more than a comrade, an airman, a partner, but she was a woman, too. One who'd been in love, who'd nearly gotten married, who'd lost her fiancé.

He started walking again, because if he let himself, he'd keep staring into her face and into her eyes, and that was no way to keep things professional.

"I learned how to make a shirt sling the summer I turned eleven," he said, determined to not feel awkward or discomfited. He liked Gretchen as an airman and a person. Noticing that she was lovely didn't mean that he'd crossed some well-marked line. It just meant that he'd noticed.

It was his job, after all, to pay attention.

He could have kept telling himself that until the cows came home, and it wouldn't have changed the fact that he'd worked with a lot of women and he'd never paid attention to their hair or eyes or skin.

"Were you one of those outdoorsy types? Always prepared for whatever happened?" she guessed.

"No. My father pulled my arm out of the socket. He popped it back in himself. He didn't want to bother with doctors and medical bills. So I made a sling out of an old shirt and used it until the shoulder felt better." It wasn't a story he'd ever shared, and he wasn't sure why he was sharing it now.

"Were you roughhousing?"

"That's one way to put it."

"So, he did it on purpose?" she asked, and he could hear the surprise in her voice.

"I wouldn't say that. He was trying to drag me into the house, and I didn't want to go."

"Oh."

"You say that as if you get it," he commented.

"I don't. I was very fortunate. My parents were and are great people, but I understand what you're not saying. And I'm sorry. It sounds like your childhood was hard."

"It could have been easier."

"You've made sure Portia's is. You're a really good dad, Justin."

"You've seen me with Portia a handful of times. You don't have much to base that on."

"She's here. Living on base with you. You could have sold her mother's house and used the money to help raise her."

"Melanie paid off the house a few months before she died. She was always really good with money," he replied, because it was the truth. They might not have worked as a couple, but he'd liked Melanie. Maybe even loved her in the way people loved long-distance family.

"All the more reason to sell it. At least, some people would think so. You could have a nice little nest egg sitting in the bank. Instead, you're paying a management company to rent the place out so that Portia can have it one day."

"That doesn't make me a good father. It just makes me a decent human being."

"Why are you so opposed to the idea that you might actually be good at parenting?" she asked.

He could tell her that his parents had been

poor examples and that he felt pretty certain he would mess up like they had, but they'd reached the cruisers, the strobe lights flashing across the pavement and nearby buildings. Three patrol officers were standing near the street, and they were as good an excuse as any to pretend he hadn't heard the question.

"I'd better go talk to them. See if they saw anything. Maybe we can get surveillance footage of the vehicle." He pointed at security cameras attached to the eaves of the corner store.

"Good thinking," she replied. "I'll go check on Portia." She took off, not running, but not walking, either.

Maybe she'd felt what he had—lines being crossed, too much personal information being exchanged.

It wasn't uncommon for partners to share the details of their lives. He'd known just about everything there was to know about Corbin's family, his childhood, his hobbies. They'd been partners when they were on duty and buddies when they weren't, and there hadn't been anything strange or awkward about it.

After Corbin was killed, Justin had worked with a few other MPs while he was training as a K-9 handler. He'd never worried that lines were being crossed with his female partners.

He'd hung out with them after work sometimes, gone to their houses for dinner if they had husbands or kids. He'd been a brother to some of them, and to some he'd just been the guy they worked with.

In all his years as an MP, he'd never wondered what would happen if he was partnered with someone he was attracted to, because he'd never expected to be attracted.

So, this strangeness with Gretchen? It had to be a glitch. A product of fatigue or adrenaline. Worrying about Portia was getting to him, and he wasn't focusing the way he should.

That had to be it, because anything else was out of the question.

She wasn't running away from Justin.

Not really.

She was running to his daughter, because someone had to check on the teenager. Sure, Portia was safe at headquarters, guarded by MPs and far away from Boyd Sullivan, but she was probably scared and worried about her father.

That was as good an excuse as any for Gretchen to hurry away. She probably should have given back Justin's shirt before she left, but all she'd been thinking about was what she'd seen in his eyes—a flash of something that reminded her of midnight walks and candlelit dinners. Girlish dreams and adolescent crushes.

If he'd been anyone else, she'd have wondered if something was growing between them, if a bond was forming that went beyond work and friendship. But Justin wasn't just anyone. He was the guy she'd worked with for months. He was the captain of the Security Forces, a man she admired for his integrity, his honesty and his love for his daughter. There couldn't be anything but work between them, because he was the kind of guy she could fall for if she let herself.

She didn't intend to let herself.

Her heart had shattered when Henry died. She'd slowly been piecing it back together again, learning to go on without him, to accept that the life they should have had would never be.

That was enough for now.

She didn't need to add a relationship into the mix. At least, not a romantic one.

Friendship was fine. If they kept things light and easy. That was how it had been for months. She had no intention of changing things.

Sometimes, though, you didn't get to choose

how life went. Sometimes you put your all into doing the right thing and being the right person, and ended up in an unexpected and unwanted situation.

Sometimes good intentions weren't enough.

Sometimes even prayer didn't seem to help.

Sometimes God's way wasn't a road that a person ever expected to travel, and all she could do was hold on tight and trust in His promises.

"But sometimes we do have the power to decide things," she muttered as she reached headquarters. "Sometimes we can stay on course. This is going to be one of those times."

Because she wasn't going to risk her heart again. Whatever direction she went after this assignment, she would be going alone.

She opened the door and stepped into the building.

This time of night, the corridors were usually empty, the MPs who were on duty out on patrol. Tonight, though, the building seemed to bustle with activity. MPs. Dogs. The constant thud of boots or pad of paws on the floor.

She strode through the hall, waving at a few MPs, but not stopping to speak to any of them. She was eager to find Portia. At sixteen, she wasn't a baby or even a young child. But she'd been through a lot, and she had to be terrified.

Gretchen approached the desk sergeant and asked what room Portia had been taken to. The MP typed information into a computer and scanned the screen. "Interrogation Room One. Do you want me to have someone take you, ma'am?"

"I'm familiar with the building and can find the room, but thank you." She stepped away, then stopped. "If Captain Blackwood reports in or radios in, let him know that I'm with his daughter."

She hurried away, walking through a set of doors and deeper into the building.

"Gretchen!" a woman called. "Hold up!"

Gretchen turned, surprised to see Felicity James and her new husband, Westley, hurrying toward her. Now a base photographer, Felicity had been a trainer with the Canyon K-9 training program her husband led. Unlike his extroverted wife, the master sergeant was quiet and somber, but he had a reputation for being a dog whisperer—the kind of trainer who could get the best out of every K-9 he trained.

She greeted Felicity and Westley as they approached. "It's good to see you. I guess you heard that Boyd Sullivan has been spotted on base again." Like all the members of the investigation team, the two had been deeply involved in trying to apprehend Boyd.

"We did," Westley responded. "But that's not why we're here. We got a call from Special Agent Oliver Davison. He has some information he wants to share and asked us to meet him here."

"This is late for a meeting," she said, and Felicity nodded.

"We're hoping he's in a hurry to meet with us because he has information about the dogs that are still missing."

It was possible. The FBI has been working to infiltrate the Olio Crime Syndicate, and the CAFB K-9 team believed the syndicate might have purchased a few of the German shepherds that had been released, including the four superstars. The well-trained, missing K-9s—Glory, Liberty and Scout—should have been easy to recall, but despite months of searching they remained missing. Two months ago, Patriot—the fourth phenomenal shepherd—had been found at the base gate wearing a collar that had been attributed to Olio. The team had asked the FBI to investigate, and Special Agent Oliver Davison had been leading the efforts.

"Do you really think that's what this is

about?" Gretchen asked, hoping for the sake of the team and the dogs that it was.

"If the dogs were, as we suspect, purchased by Olio, it's very possible," Felicity said.

"I hope they know what they've got," Westley said. "If they understand the value of the dogs, they'll take better care of them."

"Rusty knows the value of the dogs, and I'm certain if he was responsible for selling them to the crime organization, he charged an exorbitant fee." Rusty Morton was a K-9 trainer who was suspected of being responsible for the missing dogs.

"I agree, Gretchen," Felicity said. "But until we find Rusty, we have no idea whether he was actually involved."

"He was involved," Westley said, his voice hard.

"We'll let a judge and jury decide that," Felicity responded, hooking her arm through his. "We'd better get to the meeting. Are you joining us, Gretchen?"

"I will once I've checked on Portia."

"Is she here?" Felicity's eyes were wide with surprise. "I thought they'd have transported her to a safe house by now. We heard that Sullivan kidnapped her."

"He did. We need to get her statement before we move her."

"I can't believe Sullivan had the gall to walk into Justin's house."

"He didn't just walk in the house. He murdered the man Justin hired to guard Portia," Gretchen said, the image of the security guard lying on the ground suddenly filling her head. He'd been ambushed, shot from behind, not given even a fighting chance to defend himself. That was a reminder of what they were up against.

Because *that* was the kind of killer Sullivan was. No guilt. No remorse. Very few mistakes.

He'd made one tonight, though.

And she was going to pray that he continued to do so.

A criminal's mistake was a police officer's miracle. At least, that was the way she saw it.

"Another victim," Westley said grimly. "Sullivan needs to be stopped before more people die."

"We'll catch him," she assured the master sergeant.

"How many people are going to die before then, Gretchen?" he asked, rubbing the back of his neck and sighing. "Felicity is right. We need to go. See you at the meeting when you finish with Portia. If not, we'll fill you in."

"I'd appreciate that," she said as they turned to walk away. They both looked tired. The past few months had taken their toll, Sullivan's games escalating as he targeted four people he believed wronged him. Felicity was one of them. Justin was another. The stress of being in a killer's sights had to be intense.

Gretchen had come to Canyon Air Force Base to shadow Justin and to learn from him. She'd had no idea that she'd become part of a team tasked with the job of capturing an elusive serial killer. This wasn't her hometown or her territory. She had nothing but military ties to the people who lived on base, but those ties were strong.

As much as she was ready to move on with her life, to go back to Minot and make her decision about leaving the military or staying, she couldn't go until Sullivan was caught and the people she'd begun to care about were safe.

She sighed, turning a corner and walking into a narrow hall that led to the interrogation rooms. There were several unmarked doors lining the corridor. She didn't need a number to find Portia. She could hear her high-pitched voice drifting through the hallway, the words muffled.

Gretchen followed the sound to an open door. Portia was sitting at a small table in the center of the room, talking on the phone that was on the table beside her, twisting the chord as she held the receiver to her ear. Across from her, an MP sat with his legs stretched out, his arms crossed.

He jumped up as Gretchen entered the room, offering a sharp salute. "Captain, I've taken the victim's statement and filed the report."

"Thank you, Airman."

"Would you like an escort back to Captain Blackwood's house?"

"We'll stay here until he returns," she responded, not bothering to mention the safe house or the plans to move Portia there. The fewer people who had the information, the better. "You can head back to whatever you were doing. I'll take over guard duty," she added.

"Yes, ma'am." He didn't hesitate. Obviously, listening to a teenage girl's phone conversation wasn't his idea of a good time.

Gretchen lowered herself into the chair, her arm throbbing in time with her heartbeat, her head just woozy enough to make her wonder how much blood she'd lost.

Probably more than she should have.

Portia was still twirling the chord and still talking.

She met Gretchen's eyes and offered a shaky smile. "Hold on," she said. Then she covered the receiver with her hand and whispered, "I'll only be a minute."

"Take your time. We can't leave until your father gets here."

Portia nodded and went back to her conversation. Something about proms and dates and the best place to buy dresses. Maybe talking about these normal teenage topics gave Portia a sense of normalcy.

Portia finally hung up, her hand shaking as she smoothed her hair and fiddled with the sleeve of her sweater.

"Have you heard from my dad yet?" she asked without meeting Gretchen's eyes.

"Not yet, but I'm sure he'll be here soon. Was that someone from Michigan?"

"No. It was Natalie. She's in my physics class."

"So, you're friends," Gretchen said, hoping to keep the conversation going and keep Portia's mind off her father.

Portia shrugged.

"You're not?"

"Why do you care?" It was a typical teenage answer. One that Gretchen might have offered at the same age. Not meant to be particularly rude, but not meant to be polite, either.

"Because we're both sitting here, and if we don't discuss your father or Boyd Sullivan, then there's not a whole lot to talk about unless I ask questions."

Portia met her eyes and smiled. "You're not what I expected, Gretchen."

"No?"

"Most of the bodyguards Dad has left me with try to be too nice. Like I'm fragile and I might break if they aren't."

"You've been through a lot, Portia."

"Lots of people go through difficult things. Mom worked as an emergency room nurse. She saw the results of horrible things happening to people every day."

"That's a hard job."

"Maybe, but Mom loved it. She didn't care that I wasn't interested in following in her footsteps, though. She wanted me to pursue my dreams."

"Which are?"

"See? That's what I mean. You're not pretending that my life is just going to skate along for a while because my mother died. You're assuming I still have goals and dreams."

"Your life hasn't ended. It's just changed. That doesn't change you. At least, not the part of you that has goals and dreams."

"Right. Like I said, you're not like the other MPs."

"And you still haven't told me what your plans for the future are."

"I want to be a journalist."

"Is that why you started the blog?"

Portia hesitated, and Gretchen thought she might refuse to answer.

Instead, she sighed. "Maybe. I mean, I considered myself to be doing investigative reporting, but I got caught up in things and started poking the bear with a stick instead of reporting on what it was doing."

"Is that what your father said?"

"My father is really busy trying to catch the Red Rose Killer. And he doesn't want to put a wedge between us. Like, he doesn't want to come down too hard on me, because we don't know each other all that well yet. So, he hasn't said much. Except that I should haven't done it. That it was dangerous. That I made myself the killer's target. He's right about all of that, but I came up with the bear analogy myself."

"It's a good one."

"Yeah," Portia said, leaning back in the chair and sighing. "I've had a lot of time to come up with it. I haven't been allowed to leave the house alone since he found out."

"This will be over soon," Gretchen said, hoping she was right.

"Maybe. Or maybe not. Either way, I guess I'm going to some stupid safe house."

"A safe house isn't stupid," Justin said as he stepped into the room, buttoning the top button of a crisp uniform shirt.

Gretchen stood, surprised that he'd returned so quickly. Surprised, too, by the quick jump of her pulse when she looked in his eyes.

She glanced away, focusing her attention on Quinn. He looked happy, his tail thumping as he lay beside Justin.

"The idea of missing school is stupid," Portia corrected. "The idea of staying with people I don't know is stupid. The idea of being safe isn't stupid."

"I'm glad you feel that way, honey, because there's an FBI agent here, and he was able to get a safe house approved for you. We're going back to the house, and you'll have a few minutes to pack before you leave."

"Before I leave?" Portia asked. "You're not coming with me?"

"We found one of the vehicles Sullivan used, and a couple of the dogs are on his scent trail. Quinn is the best apprehension dog on the team. He needs to be out there. And so do I."

"But, Dad—"

"There's more to it than that, Portia. I'm the person Boyd is after. If he's going to watch anyone tonight, it's going to be me. I want you moved out of the way while he's distracted. I don't want him to have the slightest chance of following."

"And I don't get a say in this?" Portia asked, shoving away from the table and standing. Right then, her eyes blazing and her chin up, she looked as strong and indomitable as her father. Gretchen could imagine her in a few years—graduating from college, heading into a career as an investigative reporter. From the look of things, she had the guts for it. She also had the writing ability. Like everyone else involved in the case, Gretchen had read her blog.

"No," Justin answered firmly.

"That's totally not cool."

"I'm not going for cool. I'm going for keeping you alive."

"Fine. Whatever. Where's the person who's

taking me to the house? I want out of here." She stomped into the hall, and Justin shook his head.

"Apparently, I am exceptionally good at upsetting her," he said, talking to Gretchen but eyeing the doorway.

"At that age, everyone upset me."

"Really?" he asked, turning his light blue gaze in her direction.

She lost her train of thought, forgot what he'd said, what she'd said, what they were talking about.

This was not good.

Not at all.

"We should probably go after her. The sooner you and Quinn get on the trail, the sooner we can have Sullivan in custody," she said, because she wanted to be back on the move, back on the job. Not standing in a small interrogation room with a man who made her pulse jump.

"I'm praying we get him tonight. He needs to be stopped. Not just for Portia's sake. For everyone's. The bodyguard he murdered tonight has a family. He has people who love him." Justin shook his head, his fist clenched just like Portia's had been.

"I know, and I'm sorry."

"Me, too, but sorry isn't going to mean anything to his family. They're going to want justice, and I plan to make sure they get it. Come on. Let's head out." He strode into the hall, Quinn beside him, and Gretchen followed.

This was what she was here for.

To do a job that mattered.

To be part of a team that was dedicated to justice.

Everything else was secondary.

And the quick, hard beat of her heart when she looked into Justin's eyes?

That didn't matter at all.

SEVEN

It didn't take Portia long to pack her things.

She tore through her room, tossing clothes and books into a suitcase, grabbing a photo of Melanie from her nightstand and a Bible from her dresser. She didn't even glance in Justin's direction as she worked.

He tried not to be bothered by that.

Gretchen had said that everyone had upset her when she was Portia's age. Maybe so, but Portia didn't seem to be upset with anyone but him.

She asked Gretchen to grab a sweater from the closet, thanked an MP who offered to carry the suitcase downstairs. She even smiled at Special Agent Oliver Davison.

But Justin, she ignored.

"Are we set?" Oliver asked, his gaze skirting across the bed.

The laptop Portia had been using was gone,

along with the note. Justin knew who the perpetrator was. What they were hoping was to find some evidence of where he'd been holing up.

"I think so." Portia whirled around, grabbed another photo from her dresser. This was one that had been taken in the summer—the two of them at a church picnic. She had a sunburned nose and a broad smile. He had his arm around her shoulders.

He remembered the day and the feeling that they were finally connecting, that he was beginning to understand her. That maybe they were going to be okay.

A couple of months later, he'd learned that she was the anonymous blogger. Since then, it seemed as if they were back at square one. Tiptoeing around each other, trying to figure out the steps of a dance that neither of them had ever learned.

"If you get there and find out that you forgot something, I'll have someone bring it to you," he offered, and she finally looked at him.

Her face was pale, her eyes red-rimmed with fatigue. She looked determined, though. Stoic. Like someone who knew what had to be done and planned to do it. No matter how much she didn't want to.

He understood that.

He'd been that type of teenager.

"I don't want to do this, Dad," she said, grabbing her backpack and hoisting it onto her shoulder.

"I know."

"I don't think you do."

"Then how about you explain it to me?"

"You think I don't want to go because I don't want to be in some weird house with a bunch of people I don't know."

"It's not a weird house," Oliver offered, taking a duffel bag that Portia had filled and zipped. "It's nice. Your room is big, and you'll have a nice computer setup. No internet access, but you can play games or journal. I read your blog posts. You're a gifted writer."

"If you're trying to remind me that this is my fault, and that I wouldn't have to leave if I hadn't been so stupid, don't bother. I think about how dumb I was every day. If I could go back and *not* write the blog, I would."

"Hey, it was just a comment," Oliver said calmly. "I'm not trying to do anything but make the safe house sound like a nice place to spend some time. Which it is."

"Nice would be going back to Michigan. Nice is not going wherever we're going," she responded, turning to look at Justin. "But I'm not worried about the house or how things will be there. I'm worried about you, Dad. With Mom gone, you're all I have left. And if I'm at the safe house, I can't make sure you're okay."

"Portia—"

"I know it doesn't make sense. You're an air force captain and a military police officer, and you know how to take care of yourself." She shrugged. "But I still have this feeling that if I'm with you, you'll be safe, and if I'm not… maybe you won't be."

"You know what?" Gretchen said, stepping forward. "How about Special Agent Davison and I meet you two downstairs?"

She hurried out of the room, and Oliver followed.

Obviously, she was trying to give Justin a few minutes to say what needed to be said, to reassure Portia that he'd be okay. That she wasn't going to be left alone.

"Don't worry about it, Dad," she said before he could speak. "I'll go. I know you and Quinn have to go find Sullivan."

She would have left the room, and he could have let her go. It would have been the easy thing to do. It was what he wanted to do. He couldn't promise her he'd be okay. His job was dangerous, and every day that he did it, he took risks.

She knew that, and she wouldn't believe any platitude he might try to feed her.

But he couldn't let her go without offering some reassurance.

"Wait." He touched her arm, and she stopped.

"What?" she asked, exasperated or trying to act like she was—bangs hanging in her eyes, hand on her hip, eyes shooting daggers.

"I know you're scared."

"Glad you finally figured that one out." She started walking again.

"I'm scared, too."

She stopped.

"Not about the situation with Boyd. Not about my safety," he continued. "I'm afraid I'll mess this up. That I won't be the parent you need. That you'll finish growing up, and I still won't know your favorite color or what size shoe you wear. I've tried to be a good long-distance father—"

"You have been," she said, all her exasperation and attitude gone.

"But now it's time for me to be the kind of parent that's right in the middle of all of it. The daily problems. The school troubles. The teenage—"

"Drama?" she cut in, brushing the bangs out of her eyes.

"That wasn't quite the word I was going to use," he said, and she offered a half smile.

"It's what Mom always said. That teenage drama was going to give her a head full of gray hair."

"Your mom did a great job with you, Portia. You've turned into an intelligent, strong, independent young woman. But you still have a lot of growing up to do, and it's my job to make sure that you're safe while you do it. The easiest and best way for me to do that is to have you in a location that Boyd can't find."

"But he can still find you, Dad. What if he ambushes you or makes a bomb or hires someone to hurt you?"

"I have an entire team of people who are working with me to make sure that doesn't happen, but as long as my focus is on your safety, I'm not going to be able to concentrate like I should. You going to a safe house will keep us both safe, because it will free the part of my mind that is currently focused a hundred percent on making sure Boyd doesn't get to you."

She frowned. "I don't want to be a distraction. I just want to help keep you safe."

"So go to the safe house. Follow the rules. Cooperate with the people who will be guarding you. Trust me and the team to capture Boyd."

"And trust God to keep you safe?" she asked quietly. "I did that with Mom and look what happened."

"Sometimes we can't understand His plans, Portia. But we can always count on the fact that He'll take difficult situations and use them for our benefit. If we let Him," he responded, repeating words Corbin had said to him years ago.

"Mom used to say that, too—*God can make the toughest times into the biggest blessings.* If she were here, I'd ask how her dying could ever be that." She sniffed, a tear sliding down her cheek.

He wiped it away, pulled her into his arms. "Honey, I'm not going to pretend that I understand God's ways. But I know this—faith is never wasted. Your mother was one of the most faith-filled people I know, and she wouldn't want you to doubt God's goodness because of what happened to her," he said, knowing it was true. Justin had admired Melanie's work ethic, her drive, her parenting skills, and he'd admired her faith. She'd become a Christian after Portia's birth, and she'd never wavered from the conviction that God had used one of the hardest times in her life to show her the truth about His love.

"I don't. I just want to know that He's not going to let you be taken from me, too."

"He's not."

"Do you really believe that?" she asked.

"Yes. Like I said, faith is never wasted. Whatever happens, you're going to be okay. I promise." It was the best he could do, the most honest he could be, and he could only hope the truth was what she wanted.

She nodded, stepping away. "I know. I love you, Dad. I'll follow whatever stupid rules they have at the safe house, and I'll pray for you every day. And when this is all over, we're going to plan that trip to Michigan. Okay?"

"Okay."

"See you later, alligator." She offered the words they'd said to each other when she was in elementary school.

"In a while, crocodile," he responded, surprised and pleased that she'd remembered.

She grinned, kissed his cheek and walked away, her backpack bouncing, her shoulders straight. She was her mother's daughter.

But she was his daughter, too.

He might not have spent as much time with Portia as he'd wanted during her formative years, but he'd supported Melanie's parenting in every way he could. Not just with finances. He'd been a willing ear, a second opinion. He'd been there when Portia had ear tubes put in, and when she'd had her tonsils out. There had been dozens of times when he'd taken leave to be there for her and Melanie, and he'd like to think that the confident young woman who'd just walked out of the room had learned some of her strength from him.

Maybe his father hadn't rubbed off on him.

Maybe he *could* be what he'd wanted when he was a kid—the kind of parent who listened and who really heard, who offered support and encouragement along with the parameters for right living.

He called Quinn to heel and walked out of the room, closing the door behind him.

Gretchen had never liked goodbyes. When she was a kid, her father's air force career had meant a lot of them. Her brothers had grown up and gone into the military, and she'd found herself saying goodbye to them, too.

She preferred *hello*.

Or *see you later*.

She tried not to watch as Portia threw her arms around Justin one last time. She tried not to listen when she made him promise to be careful. But, of course, they were all standing in the foyer of Justin's house, crowded together, and she couldn't help but see and hear father and daughter say their goodbyes.

She had a lump in her throat, and she wasn't even going to pretend that she didn't.

"You'd probably better go, Captain. If Boyd is watching the team that's tracking him, he'll notice if you're not there. We don't want him to realize we're moving Portia," Special Agent Davison said, putting a hand on Portia's arm. "I'll get her to the house safely. I've got three agents there, and your team is sending in some MPs. She'll be safe."

"I'm counting on that," Justin said. "Follow the rules, Portia. It's the only way to stay safe."

"I will, Dad," she promised, sniffing back tears.

"Ready?" Gretchen asked, opening the door and letting cool air drift in. She didn't want to rush Justin, but Oliver was right. Sullivan knew the team's routines. He'd been observing them for months. If Justin wasn't around, he'd wonder why. The last thing any of them needed or wanted was for him to return to

Justin's place looking for him. If he saw Portia leaving, he'd follow. Maybe he'd be spotted. Maybe not. The guy was slick, and he was smart. He might launch an attack before the transport reached the safe house.

She frowned, stepping out into the darkness, a cold breeze ruffling her hair. She scanned the yard, her arm throbbing in time with the beat of her heart. She still had the makeshift sling Justin had given her, and she adjusted her arm to try to ease the pain.

There were still several MP vehicles parked near the curb. Yellow crime scene tape had been strung around the bushes where the bodyguard had been found. An MP was taking photos of the area, and the evidence team was still working. She'd like to think that Boyd would keep his distance. Most criminals would. But Boyd wasn't most criminals. He was a psychopath and a narcissist. A guy who believed he was too smart to be caught.

"And that's going to be your undoing," she murmured.

"What is?" Justin asked, and she swung around to face him.

"I was just thinking about Boyd's arrogance, about the fact that he doesn't believe he can be caught. That's what's going to lead to his capture."

"You're worried he's coming back here, aren't you?"

"I don't think he will while all this activity is going on, but I do think he'll be back if he doesn't see you out searching for him."

"He may be off base, Gretchen."

"Maybe, but everything I've learned about him says differently."

"What do you mean?" He walked down the porch stairs, calling for Quinn to follow.

"You're his main target, and he wants to see you suffer. Knowing that Portia is in danger is fear inducing, and Boyd is the kind of person who revels in instilling fear. He's going to want to know that he's accomplished his goal—that you're terrified for Portia, that maybe you're even losing your focus."

"If that's what he wants, he's going to be disappointed. I may be afraid for my daughter, but I haven't lost my focus," he said, popping the hatchback of his SUV and giving Quinn the signal to jump in. "Let's head out. If he is hanging around, I want to get him away from Portia."

He closed the hatch and opened her door, waiting as she climbed in.

"I know your shift ended an hour ago, Captain," he said, leaning down so they were eye-to-eye. "I can take you back to the station if you want to clock out. I don't expect you to work 24/7."

"I expect it." She buckled her seat belt.

"You got twenty-five stitches in your arm. I think a little time off is in order."

"I think the guy who caused me to get the stitches needs to be in jail, so how about we not waste time arguing about whether or not I should go home?"

"We're not arguing. I was stating a fact."

"So was I."

He stared into her eyes, and at first it was nothing. Just the two of them looking at each other. Like any other time during any other shift.

But then, she felt it again. That shift in the air, that strange feeling that they were connecting in a way she hadn't expected and didn't want.

He frowned, backing away and closing the door. Not speaking as he started the engine and pulled away from the house. They were both professionals, and they both behaved in ways that reflected that. But there was tension that hadn't been there before. Some unspoken thought that filled the space between them.

She didn't break the silence, and when they finally reached Boyd's abandoned vehicle, she was relieved.

She exited the SUV before Justin turned off the engine and hurried to the abandoned vehicle. It was a small Dodge. Two doors. Dark colored. Nondescript. The front license plate was in place, and she walked to the back of the vehicle, noting the blown-out tire.

An officer was walking around the car. Tall, with dark hair and broad shoulders, he had a bloodhound beside him.

"Lieutenant Donovan?" Gretchen called, recognizing the explosives expert and his dog, Annie, immediately.

"Captain Hill," he responded, saluting as she approached.

"Find anything interesting?"

"We didn't find explosives," he responded. "That's generally the most interesting thing to me and Annie."

"You searched the vehicle?"

"The front and back seat are clear. Console has been cleaned out. Nothing in the glove compartment. We found a single red rose in the trunk." Nick opened it, stepping back so that she could look inside.

A rose had been left there. Dark red petals. Long stem. No note, but Boyd might not have had time to leave one. He'd been on the run, but he'd still wanted them to know that he was in control.

"He was taunting us," she said, taking out her flashlight and shining the beam into the trunk's dark corners.

"He definitely wanted us to know it was him," Nick agreed.

"It's not like we had any doubt," Justin said as he joined them, Quinn at his side. The Malinois didn't approach Annie. Both were too well trained to do more than look at each other.

"I searched the cabin, your house and the empty property. Not even a hint of explosives or accelerants anywhere," Nick said. "I'm thankful for that. Put enough explosives in a residential area, and you can injure a lot of people."

"Currently, Boyd's focus seems to be on injuring just me." Justin glanced in the trunk, then walked around to the driver's door and opened it with a gloved hand. "You said the interior is empty."

"Yes. He cleaned out any identifying documents. There's no title. No insurance. Not even a crumb on a floor mat. I thought maybe he'd stolen it from a used car lot, but we ran the plates. It belongs to an airman who lives a couple of miles from here. She'd left the keys in the ignition when she went inside with some groceries. He stole it from her driveway."

"When?" Justin asked, signaling for Quinn to find the scent and search. The dog sniffed the front seat, the steering wheel and the door.

"Two nights ago," Nick replied.

"So, he's been on base and ready to take action since then." Gretchen wasn't surprised, and she wasn't happy. He'd planned the kidnapping, and he'd executed it perfectly. His error had been in playing games with Justin. Giving clues. Drawing him into the woods and assuming that he'd go there alone.

"Looks that way." Nick said something to Annie, and the bloodhound sat, her long ears swinging gently as she moved. "Now he's on the run, but I have a feeling he's not going far."

"Why do you say that?" Justin asked as Quinn sniffed the ground near the car. Nose down, tail up, he seemed to catch the scent immediately.

"I was in basic training with him, remember? He never liked a challenge. He liked things to be easy, and when they were, he bragged that it was because he was superior to the recruits who were struggling. When they weren't, he wanted to quit."

"And you think things are getting difficult for him?" Justin asked.

"Definitely. We're closing in, and he knows it. I don't think he's going to enjoy the feeling of us breathing down his neck, and he's going to be very unhappy about losing his kidnapping victim." He frowned. "Sorry. Losing your daughter, Captain."

"She was a kidnapping victim, Lieutenant. No need to dance around that, but I agree. He's been sloppier tonight. His emotions are getting the better of him."

"Emotions? I didn't think he had any," Nick said.

"Sure he does. All the dark ones—hate, anger, malice," Gretchen replied.

"Those and the need for revenge. Quinn is on the scent. We're going to see what we can find." Justin gave the command and Quinn darted forward, nearly flying down the center of the street.

Justin raced after him.

Leaving Nick and his K-9 to their work, Gretchen followed, adrenaline pumping through her, thoughts focused. All her worries about Justin were gone. There was nothing in her head right now but the mission and the goal: find Boyd Sullivan and take him into custody.

They searched for hours, working their way from one street to the next. When Quinn lost the trail, they worked a grid pattern, covering several miles of the business district before heading into the residential area.

But the trail had gone cold, and finally Justin called Quinn to heel.

Gretchen didn't plan to admit it, but she was glad. Her arm had been throbbing for hours, the pain intensifying as the night wore on.

"We'd better call it," Justin said wearily. "He's slipped through our fingers again."

"Tomorrow is a new day," she replied, too tired to think of anything profound or uplifting. She was disappointed, too. They'd been close to capturing Boyd in the cabin. Maybe closer than anyone had ever been.

"It *is* tomorrow," he responded. "The sun will be up in a couple of hours. How about we go back to headquarters, file our report and get a couple of hours' sleep?"

She nodded, then thought better of it. "Unless you think we missed something at the cabin or at your place. A clue that will lead us to his hiding place."

"The evidence team is exceptional. If there was something to find, they'd have found it." They'd reached the street where Boyd had abandoned his car. It was quiet now. No sign of Nick and Annie. No sign of Boyd's vehicle.

"Looks like they've already impounded the Dodge," she commented as they reached Justin's SUV.

"The team is trying to process evidence quickly and thoroughly. We're all hoping something was missed during the initial search."

"Like what? A map with an X marking Boyd's hideout?"

Justin grinned, his face softening with amusement as he opened the hatch and let Quinn jump in. "Wouldn't that be nice?"

"It would be," she replied, sliding into the passenger seat, her cheeks hot for reasons she refused to acknowledge. It wasn't a crime to notice Justin's smile, how handsome it made him, and there was nothing criminal about thinking he should do it more often.

"What's the plan? Aside from both of us getting a few hours of sleep?" she asked, determined to keep the conversation flowing. No more awkward silences. No more unspoken thoughts. They'd been working together for months, and there'd never been any of that before.

Nothing had changed.

Nothing was going to change.

She'd make sure of it.

"Both of us staying alive." He started the engine and pulled into the road.

"Good plan, Captain. Now, how about we go into the details of how that's going to happen?"

"You could go back to Minot," he suggested, and that was enough to chase any thought about his smile out of her head.

"You're kidding."

"No. I'm not," he said.

"I can't cut my training short," she replied.

"I can speak to your commanding officer. I'm sure your safety is his priority."

"His priority is launching a K-9 MP team on base. My safety, like the safety of every airman under his command, is a matter of God's grace and my ability to do my job well." The words were stiff, but she managed to keep emotion from her voice.

"You're angry," he guessed. "And that wasn't my intention."

"Of course I am. You've seen me work. You know I'm good at my job. Yet, somehow, you don't think I'm capable of helping you solve the Red Rose Killer case."

"We're not solving anything." He pulled into the parking lot at headquarters and parked his vehicle close to the front door. "We're chasing a killer. One who would put a bullet in your head as quickly as he would mine."

"And?"

"I want you out of here, Gretchen." He turned off the engine and turned to face her. "Not because you're not capable. Because Boyd will hurt anyone he thinks matters to me."

"We're work partners. Not—"

He raised his hand, cutting off the words.

"The truth isn't going to matter to Boyd, and I'm not willing to lose another partner. I want you to go back to your assignment in Minot. I'll tell your commanding officer that I've taught you everything I can."

"Lose *another* partner? What does that mean?" she asked, and he tensed.

"It's not open for discussion."

"You're the one who brought it up," she pointed out.

"And now I'm shutting it down."

"You know that I can find out, right? Easily."

"Why would you want to?"

"Because you're trying to send me back to Minot before I finish my assignment here, and I want to know why."

"I'm not trying to send you anywhere. I'm making a suggestion. For your safety."

"You mentioned speaking to my commanding officer," she retorted, frustrated and unable to hide it. "I'm not Portia. I don't need your protection."

"I am very aware of that," he muttered.

"Then stop trying to keep me from doing my job."

"Your only job here was to learn. You've done that." He climbed out of the SUV and released Quinn from his crate.

She thought the conversation was over, that her frustration would continue to simmer. *Good.* She shouldn't like Justin as much as he did. She needed to start viewing him in the light of his flaws rather than his strengths. But that went against the grain. She liked to find the good in people and focus on that, but it was for the best.

"This isn't something I talk about often," he said as he hooked Quinn to his leash, "but you have a right to know since it's impacting our relationship."

We don't have a relationship, she almost

said, because she wanted to remind them both of that.

She kept her mouth shut. Something any of her four brothers would have been surprised by. She wasn't known for keeping her thoughts to herself. She'd been raised to speak the truth, and she'd found her bluntness to be an asset in the military where she seemed to be in a constant battle to prove herself to her male counterparts.

"My first partner was killed in the line of duty," Justin continued. "We'd been working together for four years. Corbin trained me. He mentored me. I spent holidays at his place, and his family became mine. His wife was like the sister I never had. His kids were like nieces and nephews. And Corbin was my brother. In every way that mattered."

"Justin, you really don't have to tell me this," she said, because she knew where this was going. She knew how the story would end, and she could already feel her heart breaking for Justin and for the family Corbin had left behind.

"You asked, Gretchen, so I'm going to tell you. Corbin and I responded to a domestic violence call. The airman who was involved had a son who played football with Corbin's oldest son. He and Corbin had seen each other at sporting events. They'd talked a few times."

"Corbin thought he wasn't violent?"

"I don't know. I've never figured it out. He got out of the car and was heading for the front door before we'd discussed any kind of strategy. He rang the doorbell, and the suspect fired on him through the door."

"I'm sorry, Justin," she said, her voice breaking on his name.

She hated that sound of weakness, hated that he'd heard it.

The last thing she wanted him to do was view her as weak or emotional. She'd worked hard to attain a reputation for being tough, reasonable and strong.

He studied her face, his light-colored eyes nearly glowing in the exterior building lights. He had chiseled features and a strong physique, but she'd seen the softness in his face when he looked at his daughter. And when he smiled.

"I'm not going to cry, if that's what you're wondering," she managed to say in her best annoyed-younger-sister voice.

She didn't feel like his younger sister, though, and maybe that was the problem. She'd begun to see him as a man rather than an air force captain.

"Everyone cries, Gretchen. Even the most hardened soldier. But I didn't give you the information to make you sad. I didn't give it to you to make you sorry. I gave it to you because I want you to understand my position. I spent years after Corbin's death asking myself if I could have saved him, wondering if I could have prevented his death by walking to the door ahead of him or insisting that we go around the back of the property."

"You couldn't have," she said.

"At this point, it doesn't matter. What matters is making sure it doesn't happen again."

"I'm not Corbin, Justin. And I'm not planning on dying. If I do, it won't be your fault. I'm glad you shared the story. It does help me understand, but it doesn't change anything. I still plan to stay for the entirety of my temporary orders. I'm going to start our report. See you inside."

She strode across the parking lot, telling herself that nothing had changed between them. She knew it was a lie.

Personal stories were great. She'd shared lots of them with coworkers, but the story Justin had told was one that defined him. It had been a catalyst that had shaped and changed the airman he'd been into the captain he'd become.

He didn't have to say that for her to understand it. She'd heard the pain and regret in his voice, and she'd understood just how deeply the grief and guilt had gone. She'd struggled with the same since Henry's death. She'd gone to a therapist, who'd told her that holding on to guilt wouldn't bring Henry back and would only stunt her ability to be in other fulfilling relationships. Gretchen still hadn't been able to let go.

Deep in her heart, she believed that a person should always be able to save the people she loved. Even knowing in her head that it wasn't true couldn't change the way she felt.

She opened the door and stepped into headquarters, her heart heavy. She'd wanted to do more than tell Justin she was sorry. She'd wanted to explain that she understood. That she lived with the same guilt and the same regret, but they were getting dangerously close to crossing boundaries they shouldn't.

She wasn't sure how she felt about that.

She liked Justin. A lot. She respected him.

And hearing his story? It had made her feel close to him in a way she hadn't before.

"Gretchen!" someone called.

She turned and was surprised to see the base

nutritionist, Yvette Crenville, standing in the cafeteria doorway.

"Yvette! What are you doing here?" she asked.

Yvette smiled. Tall, with blond hair and delicate features, she was as pretty as she was sweet.

"I work here."

"Not at this time of day."

"I heard there'd been another Boyd sighting, and I figured you'd all be out working. I wanted to make sure you had nutritious snacks when you returned. I made dark chocolate oatmeal bars. Interested?"

"You said the word *chocolate*, so I'm definitely in."

Yvette giggled. "Good. Great. I set up a table. There are a few different types of juices, too. Coffee, if you must. Decaf if you want to sleep."

"It sounds like you thought of everything."

"I try." She glanced toward the exterior door. "Did you find him?" she whispered.

"Boyd?"

"Who else?"

"Not yet."

Yvette's face fell, and she rubbed the back of

her neck. "That's too bad. I was really hopeful that this nightmare was finally going to end."

"I think we all were."

"Captain Blackwood more than any of us, I'm sure. I heard Boyd kidnapped his daughter."

"He did," Gretchen responded. Yvette worked at headquarters, creating and prepping nutritional meals. She wasn't part of the team that had been going after Boyd, but she was apparently one of his targets. She'd dated him during basic training and publicly broken up with him. Months ago, she'd received a red rose. Since then, she'd been cautious and nervous.

"Wow! That poor girl. She's just a kid. You'd think Boyd would find it in his heart to leave her alone."

"I'm not sure Boyd has a heart," Gretchen said.

Yvette tensed, her angelic features suddenly pinched and tight. "Everyone has a heart."

"It was a joke, Yvette. Not meant to be taken literally."

"Right. Sorry." Yvette rubbed the back of her neck again and smiled sheepishly. "My parents always told me I was much too literal. I do understand what you're saying. Boyd is rotten to the core. I can't believe I dated him during basic training. He was a total dud. The kind of guy that only wants to be with someone he can use." There was a hint of venom in her voice.

She didn't look angry, though.

She looked sweet and placid and eager to please.

Gretchen wasn't buying the facade. She'd met people who really were as sweet and kind as they seemed, but something about Yvette rubbed her the wrong way. Maybe it was how she seemed to show up every time the Red Rose Killer case heated up. Maybe it was the subtle changes in her facial expression when she was talking about Boyd.

The two *had* dated.

According to people who'd been there, Yvette had made a show of breaking up, but that didn't mean her feelings for Boyd had died. A couple of months ago, Gretchen and another team member, nurse Vanessa Gomez, had followed Yvette, watching her every move, trying to see if she and Boyd were together.

They'd found nothing out of the ordinary.

Yvette did what everyone did—shopped, went to work, went to the gym, went to church. No secret side trips into the woods. No suspicious excursions off base. No packages delivered to her house or tossed into Dumpsters. Nothing that would indicate she was aiding and abetting a criminal.

But looks could be deceiving, and Gretchen wasn't convinced Yvette was as innocent as she appeared to be. Since she had nothing but her gut to go on, she'd been keeping quiet and staying alert. Eventually, every criminal made a mistake. If Yvette were somehow aiding Boyd, she'd be found out.

"What?" Yvette asked, smoothing her hair and swiping at her cheek. "You're staring at me like I have something on my face."

"No. I was just thinking about your relationship with Boyd."

"That was a long time ago." Yvette laughed nervously. "It was destined to fail from the beginning. He loved fast food." She shuddered. "Who would put junk like that into his body?"

"I might," Gretchen responded honestly.

"Oh! I hope not. I know you're not thirty yet, but you know what happens to women when they reach that age, right? The metabolism slows, fat starts to build up, the thyroid begins to struggle. What you want to be doing is detoxing every first week of the month. Follow that with the eighty-twenty approach to eating. You remember that, right?"

How could she forget? Yvette mentioned it every time she saw Gretchen with anything that smacked of unhealthy. "Yes. I do."

"I can go over it with you again, Gretchen. What we put into our bodies is so important to our health."

The exterior door opened, and Justin entered the building with Quinn.

"There's Justin… I mean, Captain Blackwood. I'd better run," Gretchen said, turning on her heel and nearly flying back down the hall.

Justin saw her coming and offered a quick smile that made her heart skip a beat.

"Everything okay?" he asked, his gaze shifting to Yvette and then back to Gretchen.

"We were talking about the eighty-twenty eating plan and detox," she whispered.

"Poor you," he said in a rumble of laughter.

"You don't know the half of it. I seem to be her favorite target. Last week, she cornered me two times to tell me that healthy eating was imperative as I reach middle age."

"Middle age? You're nowhere near middle age!"

"Maybe you should tell her that," she murmured, glancing over her shoulder. Yvette was still at the cafeteria door, smiling in their direction.

"I made dark chocolate oatmeal squares, Captain Blackwood," she called. "I've set up a nice snack table for your officers. Make sure you get something to eat. It looks like you've had a long night."

"Thanks, Yvette. I'll do that," he said.

He touched Gretchen's shoulder. "Ready?"

"Sure," she replied, allowing him to steer her back toward Yvette.

She could feel the warmth of his fingers through her shirt. Could feel the way her heart responded to his light touch. She could have moved away. Maybe she should have, but it had been a long day, a long few months. Really, it had been a long few years, and it felt nice to have Justin's hand on her shoulder.

She let it stay while they walked past Yvette and entered the cafeteria. A few MPs were there, milling around a table set with trays of cookie bars and pitchers of juice.

One of the MPs glanced their way, his gaze going to Justin's hand before shifting to Gretchen's bandaged arm. Finally, his attention drifted away, and he grabbed a cookie, munching it while he talked to one of his buddies.

He'd probably forget what he'd seen before he left the cafeteria. And why wouldn't he? It wasn't uncommon for military comrades to pat one another on the arm or shoulder. Hugs and back claps weren't unheard-of, and offering support was common even among airmen of differing genders.

But gossip ran rampant on military bases, and Gretchen didn't want to be fodder for the rumor mill.

She stepped away, nearly running to the table. She grabbed a napkin and two of the treats, but didn't bother trying to pour juice into a cup. Her left arm ached, and she doubted she could coordinate the movement without help. She wasn't going to ask any lower-ranking airman, and she wasn't going to ask Justin.

"I'm heading into the office," she announced a little too loudly, and then she nearly sprinted out the door and up the stairs. It might have been childish to run away, but the alternative was sticking it out and faking comfort in what had become an uncomfortable situation. Not because of anything Justin had done, but because of her own traitorous heart.

As much as she wanted to deny it, to protest it, she had to face the truth: she was attracted to Justin Blackwood.

But it—they—could never be.

“Get your act together, Hill,” she muttered, dropping into her desk chair and turning on her computer. Writing reports was her least favorite part of the job, but right now, it was the perfect excuse to keep her head in the game and off the blue-eyed captain.

EIGHT

The sanctuary was silent when Justin walked into Canyon Christian Church. Not surprising. He was a half hour early, his dress shoes spit polished and squeaking as he walked to the front of the church and took a seat in a pew. He hadn't slept well the last few nights, and he'd been up before dawn, following his Sunday morning routine, hoping that Boyd would make the mistake of coming after him. He was prepared for it, even praying for it, as he'd run his normal five-mile route and sat on the front porch with his coffee.

Daring Boyd.

Taunting him the way Boyd had taunted the team.

But, of course, Boyd hadn't shown up, and Justin had finally given up and showered. During the months that Portia had been living with him, he'd gotten into the habit of making a hot breakfast before church. It was the one morning they were both free. No school. No work. No obligations other than to themselves.

With Portia gone, there'd been no reason to cook, and he'd found himself with a little too much time on his hands. The house was empty without Portia. No music drifting from her room. No muffled complaints as she picked through the clothes in her closet or attempted to style her hair.

He hadn't realized how much those things had filled the house and made it into a home.

"I guess I'm not the only one who couldn't sleep." Gretchen's voice echoed in the empty space, and Justin turned, surprised and pleased to see her walking up the aisle. She wore a dress. Light blue and soft looking, it clung to her slender curves and fell just past her knees. No high heels. No makeup. She was beautiful, and he wasn't sure why he hadn't noticed before.

He'd seen her at church many times.

He'd seen her on base, wearing jeans and sweaters or running gear. Always with perfect skin and dark lashes and a half smile on her face, but all he'd noticed was Gretchen. The woman he worked with, partnered with, brainstormed with.

She wasn't smiling now.

She looked tired and a little unsure. That surprised him. From the day she'd arrived on base, Gretchen had been confident and filled with energy. She threw herself into her work, never seeming to doubt her abilities.

She slid into the pew beside him, setting her Bible next to her hip.

"You miss Portia," she said before he could offer a greeting.

"The house is too quiet without her."

"I'm sure. I remember when I finally moved into my own place. It was difficult getting used to the silence. Even when it was just me and my parents at home, there'd been noise and people to fill the emptiness. They entertained a lot, and it always seemed like we had someone staying at our place. Then, suddenly, I was on my own, coming home to a house that no one was in, and it felt very empty and lonely," she said as she tried to shrug out of her jacket. It caught on her bandaged arm, and he helped her, tugging gently until she was free.

"You mentioned four brothers the night you were shot. Your parents' home must have been really busy."

"First of all, I was grazed by a bullet. Not shot," she corrected.

He nodded, conceding the point. "How's the arm?"

"You've asked me that a hundred times since the incident, Justin. My answer remains the same. It's fine." She touched her arm. The sleeve of her dress covered the bandage, but he could see it bulging beneath the fabric. "And you're right. The houses I grew up in were loud. My brothers were nearly teenagers by the time I came along. They always had friends over and they kept my parents on their toes. It was a fun childhood. Loud, busy and crazy. But fun. Especially with the Ping-Pong table in the basement and a rock climbing wall in our backyard."

"You're kidding?"

"About the rock climbing wall? Nope. It's still there. My nephews and nieces love it." She dug into her purse and pulled out her phone, scrolling through until she found a photo she wanted to show him. "See?"

She handed him the phone, her cool fingers sliding across his warmer ones, and he wanted to capture her hand, look into her eyes, ask her what was wrong. Because something was.

He studied the photo—three kids and an older gentleman standing near a rock wall. All of them smiling. One of the girls looked like

Gretchen—dark hair, dark eyes, slim body and wide smile.

"She looks like you," he commented, handing the phone back.

"She's my oldest brother's kid, and he always says she looks and acts just like me. He especially says it when she's getting into trouble. Which she apparently does often." She smiled, dropping the phone into her purse. "She's nine. I keep telling him it's the age and the fact that she has three older brothers."

"Lots of boys in your family."

"Yes. I was the first girl in three generations on my dad's side. There were major celebrations when I was born. Followed by major disappointment when my grandmother realized I was a tomboy."

"Was your mother disappointed?"

"No. My mother has always given me a hundred percent support in my choices. As long as they aren't illegal or immoral, she's happy."

"It sounds like you have a great family."

"I do. I've been missing them a lot lately."

"Are they back in Minot?"

"Upstate New York. My parents grew up there, and after I was born, they bought a house near his parents. My dad was an MP for most of his air force career. We moved a lot, and he and my mom wanted us to have a home base. For a while, it was just a place to stay when we were visiting family. Now it's their year-round home. Henry and I—" She frowned. "Sorry. Not work-appropriate conversation."

"We're not at work."

"But we're coworkers, Justin."

"Is that what this is about?" he asked.

"What?"

"Whatever is bothering you."

"Who said something was?"

"We've worked together for months, Gretchen. We've spent hundreds of hours together. I know you."

"You know Captain Gretchen Hill. There's a difference." She crossed her arms over her stomach and stared at the front of the church. If she hoped the pastor would appear and begin the service, she was going to be disappointed. They were still twenty minutes from the start of the service. People would begin trickling in soon. Until then, Justin and Gretchen were alone, and he wasn't planning to stop asking questions. Tension was never good for a team, and unspoken issues had a way of festering.

"You *are* Captain Gretchen Hill. I may not know the private details of your life, but I know that you like your coffee black and your work station neat. I also know that you run every morning and have a fondness for sweets and french fries. You're a straight shooter. Which I like. You're tough. You don't put up with fools. You don't party on the weekends, and you're wondering if you want to keep working as an MP or if you're ready to leave the military and do something different."

She met his eyes and frowned. "Who told you that?"

"Which part?"

"The part about me wondering if I should leave the military."

"No one."

"Then why would you say it?"

"Am I wrong?"

She shrugged, the fabric of her dress pulling taut across her narrow shoulders.

"So, I'm right," he pressed, because he wanted to know. If Gretchen was struggling with making the decision, if she was struggling with the job, if she felt life was passing while she worked a job she no longer loved, he wanted to help her figure things out, come up with a plan, create a future that she could be happy with.

"Why does it matter, Justin? I'm going back

to Minot in a few weeks. We'll both move on with our lives, and whatever I decide to do, it won't matter to you one way or another."

For some reason, her blunt and truthful statement rubbed him the wrong way. He didn't bother hiding his irritation.

"If you think that, you don't know me very well."

"That's the point. We don't know each other. We have a working relationship, and that's all either of us wants."

"I don't recall being asked if that's what I want." He was irritated by her assumptions. That he didn't care deeply about the people he worked with. That he wouldn't bother following up and keeping in contact with them. That he'd never be interested in more than a professional relationship with someone like her.

She was intelligent, funny and driven. She worked harder than just about any MP he knew. There wasn't anyone on the team who didn't enjoy spending time with her. Male. Female. K-9. She was charismatic without trying, drawing people to her without effort.

A person would have to be blind not to notice.

He wasn't blind. He wasn't hard-hearted. He wasn't so consumed by work that he didn't think about long-term relationships. If he were a different kind of person, with a different kind of background, he'd absolutely be thinking about Gretchen in more than a professional way. There was no military rule about dating someone of the same rank, and he knew plenty of men and women who had done it, fallen in love and gotten married.

Happily-ever-after happened. Even in the military.

It just wasn't going to happen for him.

"I wasn't trying to be rude, Justin. I'm just being...practical," she said, smoothing her dress over her thighs, her fingers trembling.

"You're nervous," he said, lifting her hand and giving it a gentle squeeze. He should have released it immediately, but they were side by side, inches away from one another, and he could see the confusion and fear in her eyes. "Why?"

"This has never happened before," she replied.

"Nothing has happened."

"Not to you," she muttered.

"Not to either of us. We're sitting in an empty church having a conversation about your decision to leave the military or continue in it."

"I haven't even spoken to my family about that." She slipped her hand from his. "It's not something I'm ready to share."

"I'd think with a family like yours, you could share anything," he said, thinking about that picture—the obviously happy kids and their grandfather. No bruised cheeks. No tears. No angry scowls. They were what he'd wanted to be when he was a kid.

"In theory, yes. I should be able to share anything. But I come from a long line of military heroes. My father served as an MP for thirty years before he retired. My older brothers are all career military. My grandfather was. My grandmother was a navy nurse. The list goes on."

"I don't know your family, but I doubt they're going to boot you out of the fold if you decide you've had enough of military life."

"They won't. I just don't want to disappoint anyone. Especially not myself. The thing is, I always wanted to be an MP, to follow in my father's and brothers' footsteps. My mother was a teacher, and that seemed so boring in comparison that I stood on a chair at my ninth birthday party and announced that I planned to follow in my father's footsteps. I even put my hand on my heart." She smiled at the memory. "My father has the video of it."

He laughed, imagining her as a child earnestly insisting that she was going into the military. "I'd like to see that one day."

"Trust me, if you ever meet him, that'll be the first thing he drags out. Anyway, I made the announcement, and I never stopped believing it was going to happen. I had it in my mind that I was going to join the military and spend my life devoted to being the best MP I could. Then I met Henry in basic training, and everything changed. Suddenly, I wasn't just thinking about a career, I was thinking about a family. Kids. All the stuff that was difficult when I was growing up in a military family."

"You wanted something different?" he asked, and she nodded.

"I wanted my kids to have friends that they didn't leave every few years, and a mom who wasn't away more than she was home. Henry and I had everything planned out, and I had a whole timeline worked out in my head, and then he was diagnosed with cancer."

"That had to be devastating for both of you."

"I think I was more heartbroken than he was. He had this unbelievable faith that God was in control, and that he had nothing to worry about. He died a few weeks before our wedding, and I still haven't figured out what I want to do with the rest of my life."

The door at the rear of the sanctuary opened, and a group of parishioners walked in, laughing and talking as they made their way into the church.

He wanted to continue the conversation, but Gretchen seemed finished, her focus on the empty pulpit, her hands fisted in her lap.

Whatever boundary she'd set for their relationship, she seemed to think she'd crossed it. Her muscles looked so tense he thought they'd snap if she tried to move.

"Relax," he whispered in her ear. "I'm not the enemy, and I'm not going to use your secrets against you."

"You shouldn't know my secrets," she hissed. "I'm not even sure why I told you any of that."

"Because we're friends?"

She met his eyes. "We are, Justin, and I really value that. So let's try not to ruin things."

He would have asked what she meant, but the sanctuary was filling now, and Pastor Harmon appeared, walking through a doorway to the left. He waved at Justin and Gretchen, hurrying toward them and offering a greeting.

"How are you, Gretchen? Is the arm healing up?"

"It's nearly good as new, Pastor," she responded, and he smiled.

"Good. That's what I like to hear. And how about Portia, Justin? I heard she's been taken off base."

"She's in a safe location until Boyd Sullivan is caught."

"Poor kid. I know she's had quite an adjustment this past year. Is she okay? Is there anything my wife and I can do for her?"

"Just pray for her. I know she'd appreciate it."

"Of course, and if you need anything while she's gone, let us know. I'm sure the house is quiet without her in it."

"It is," he agreed, imagining going home after church to the emptiness. Making lunch without her sitting at the table. Spending a long day alone.

Which was something he'd done hundreds of times before.

It felt different now. It felt like a loss.

"My wife and I always have room at the table for a few friends. Why don't the two of you have lunch with us?" Pastor Harmon said as if he'd read Justin's mind.

"As much as I appreciate the offer," Justin said, "I think it would be safer for your family if I stayed away."

"Safer…? Oh. Right. Boyd. Don't worry about him, Justin. God is in control, and we trust His divine protection."

"I'd still feel better staying away, Pastor."

"And I'd feel better knowing that you weren't going home to an empty house," Pastor Harmon responded.

"I've gone home to an empty house hundreds of times. I'll be fine."

"How about you, Gretchen? We'd love to have you."

"I'll have to take a rain check, too. I have some work that needs to be done at my apartment, and today is the only day I have free."

"What kind of work?" Justin asked as the pastor stepped up to the pulpit.

"My mother sent me the supplies to make four hundred wedding favors for my brother's wedding."

"Wedding favors?"

"Yeah. The cheap little gifts the bride and groom give to their guests?"

He laughed at the description. "Sounds like something everyone wants to go home with."

"I think half the guests leave them behind,

but it's a tradition, and since it's not my wedding, I'm not going to argue with it."

"So, your brother is having four hundred guests, and you're making a gift for each of them? That sounds like a lot of work. When's the wedding?"

"New Year's Eve."

"That's right around the corner."

"Yeah. I know. The wedding favors are jars of candy kisses. Each one has to have a personalized note attached that reads *'Hugs and Kisses from the Mr. and Mrs.'*"

He laughed. He couldn't help himself. "That's..."

"Corny? Yeah. I agree."

"How did you get roped into making them?"

"My brother Micah is at Goodfellow Air Force Base. The wedding is going to be at the chapel there. Shelby—his fiancée—is finishing a residency at a hospital in Massachusetts and won't be down here until right before the ceremony. Since I'm in Texas, my mother thought it would be easier for me to make them and transport them to San Angelo than for Shelby to have to transport them from New England."

"That worked out nicely for Shelby."

"I don't mind. Shelby is a great person, and

I'm really happy she's marrying my brother. But things have been busy here, and I'm behind. Today is the day, though. I'm getting the favors done so poor Shelby has one less thing to worry about." She grabbed a hymnal and stood as the pastor invited the congregation to sing the opening hymn.

He joined her, leaning close and whispering, "Since I'm the reason you've been so busy, I'll help you with the favors."

"That's not necessary."

"Yes, it is."

"Justin—"

"Shh. You wouldn't want the old ladies in the next pew over to start frowning the way they do when the pastor's son is too loud."

She laughed and didn't continue the argument.

She might have thought he was joking, that there was no way he was planning to go to her house and spend the afternoon making wedding favors. If so, she was going to be surprised. He hadn't been joking. He might not know anything about wedding favors, but he knew four hands working a task were better than two.

He also knew that spending time with Gretchen seemed like something he wouldn't mind doing a lot more of.

* * *

They'd spent six hours making wedding favors. Six hours talking and laughing. Six hours that Gretchen refused to regret. She liked Justin. She enjoyed his company, and she was glad he'd insisted on helping out. Jobs were more fun when done with friends.

And that was what he'd said at the church.

That they were friends.

She could handle that. She could even appreciate it.

Being raised in a military family had meant making and losing friends often. She'd always been outgoing, and the process of meeting new people had never been difficult.

So, yeah. Calling Justin a friend was a natural extension of her life story.

Making sure he stayed in that category? That might be more difficult. He was too easy to talk to, too comfortable to be with. When she was around him, she forgot that her heart was broken. She forgot it needed to be protected. She forgot that loving someone meant risking losing him.

She packed a favor into the last unfilled box, tucking it in carefully. The label was completely dry, the handwritten calligraphy unsmudged.

"These looks great," Justin said, handing

her another jar. He'd filled it with chocolate kisses and screwed on the lid and wrapped a ribbon around it. "Your calligraphy skills are impressive."

"I'll have to tell my ninth-grade art teacher you said so. He was a master at it, and I wanted to learn, so he taught me."

"I'm sure you're regretting it right about now." He gestured at the boxes of favors that sat against the living room wall.

"A cramp in my hand is a small price to pay for my brother and sister-in-law's happiness," she deadpanned.

"I hear that fresh air is good for hand cramps," he said, handing her the last favor.

"Really?" She chuckled.

"No, but how about we take Quinn for a walk, anyway? Maybe grab a coffee. There's a place right around the corner."

She could think of a dozen reasons why that would be fun, and she couldn't think of one reason to refuse.

"Quinn would enjoy it," Justin added, and the Malinois lifted his head, his ears twitching. They'd picked him up after church, and he'd seemed content to lay on the floor or stare out the window. Now, though, he looked eager to get up. Get out. Do something. His tail thumped as Justin grabbed his leash and hooked it to his collar.

"I can't say no now. He'd be too disappointed." She grabbed her coat from the closet and handed Justin his. He was still wearing his dress clothes—black slacks and a blue shirt that matched his eyes. Polished shoes. He'd taken his tie off when he'd arrived, and his hair was mussed from running his hands through it.

Her palm itched to smooth the strands.

She handed him his jacket instead, opening the apartment door and stepping into the corridor.

Justin's phone rang as they walked to the elevator, and he answered quickly. "Hello? Yes."

He glanced at Gretchen and mouthed, *Ava Esposito.*

"Do you have GPS coordinates?… Send them to me and clear out. Don't go in. If Rusty is there, Sullivan could be there, too… Yeah. You're right. Olio's operatives are probably more likely. I still want you to stand down and wait for backup to arrive."

"Rusty Morton?" Gretchen asked, her heart thumping wildly.

He nodded, stepping away from the elevator and pulling her back to her apartment as he finished his conversation with Ava.

She unlocked the apartment door and ushered him in, leaving him in the living room as she ran to gear up. If Rusty had been spotted, she'd need to be ready to go to work.

The team was eager to speak with him about the still-missing dogs. Like many on the case, she felt confident he'd somehow been involved in their disappearance. She wanted to know where he'd taken them, whether he'd sold them to the Olio Crime Syndicate and where they were currently located.

She wanted them returned.

The three missing German shepherds were financially valuable, but they had intrinsic value, as well. They'd been part of Canyon Air Force Base since they were puppies, and they needed to be returned home.

It didn't take long to change into her uniform, take her service weapon from her gun safe and grab her backpack. As always, she kept it ready with water, food rations and a first-aid kit, along with everything she needed to stay warm and start a fire. Extra ammunition. Tactical gear. She wouldn't need all of it on this mission, but she didn't have time to repack.

She ran into the kitchen, grabbing a box of

dog treats she kept for Quinn and other K-9 guests and shoving them into the pack.

"What are you doing?" Justin asked.

"Preparing. If Rusty is around, it's possible some of the missing dogs are, too."

"I hope so. I'm ready to reunite them with their military family. I'm also hoping to see Scout again. He's a phenomenal K-9. I'd love for you to get a chance to meet him." He scratched Quinn's head. "Ready to work, boy?"

The dog barked once, rushing to the door and staring at Justin expectantly.

"Looks like you are," he commented. "I need to stop by my house and grab my gear, Gretchen. I'm not sure what we're going to find, but I'm going to assume we won't be walking into a friendly situation."

"Where are we heading?"

"A cave. From what Ava said, it's off the beaten track. She was out hiking with Roscoe and heard someone walking through the woods. She thought it was Boyd and took cover. When Rusty appeared, she decided to follow him rather than attempt apprehension."

"And he led her to a cave?"

"Ava said it's really hard to see. If she hadn't

watched Rusty walk into it, she's not sure she would have known it was there."

"Should I radio in for backup?"

"No. I want to keep radio silence. Just in case."

She didn't ask what he meant. She knew he was worried about a leak, concerned that someone might be feeding information to the enemy.

She understood the concern. Boyd was smart, but the way he slipped through every trap they'd set for him was uncanny and defied logic. "We could make some phone calls."

"It's Sunday evening, Gretchen. If we start pulling people away from their families and activities, the community is going to notice."

"How about Oliver Davison? We don't have any worries about the FBI being tied to Boyd or to Olio, and most people on base aren't familiar with him," she said. "I could give him a call. If we're right about Rusty selling dogs to Olio, it's possible he's meeting some of their operatives."

"Give him a call, and let's hope that's what's going on. If we can catch a few high-level Olio operatives, we might be able to bring the entire organization down."

"That would be a good day's work," she said,

pulling out her phone and dialing Davison's number as they hurried into the hall and onto the elevator.

NINE

The sun set early this time of year, and by the time Justin changed into his military uniform and grabbed his tactical gear, it was dusk, the sky dark with evening clouds. Raindrops splattered the windshield, and he turned on the wipers. A storm would be a blessing—the sound of falling rain and thunder masking their approach to the cave.

He was curious to find out why Rusty was at the caves.

The dog trainer had been missing from base for a couple of weeks. He wasn't suspected of freeing the dogs, and if he'd stuck around and answered some questions, he'd probably have been removed from the person-of-interest list. After all, the team had no doubt that Boyd was responsible for the deaths of the two trainers who'd been at the kennels the night the dogs were released, and they were certain he'd been the one to let the dogs go. The team had planned to question Rusty regarding his whereabouts that night.

But he'd run. Innocent people generally didn't do that.

They usually assumed that justice would prevail, that truth would win, and that no matter what the authorities believed, their innocence would be proven.

Rusty had gone into hiding, and he'd had a reason.

Justin was eager to find out what it was.

If, somehow, the trainer was connected to Olio, it was possible the FBI would use him to close down the crime ring.

"What are you thinking?" Gretchen asked as he pulled into the lot where Ava had left her vehicle. He could see it—a white SUV parked beneath a streetlight. He pulled up beside it and parked, switching off the ignition and turning to face Gretchen. They'd spent the afternoon together—laughing and making labels for jars of candy. Talking. Sharing. And now they were going to spend the evening bringing in criminals.

Something about that felt right and good, as if all the pieces of his life had finally come together.

He wanted to tell Gretchen that, but time

was ticking, and Ava was in the woods, waiting for backup to arrive.

That had to be his focus and his priority.

"I'm thinking that this is the break we've been waiting for."

"Are we going to wait for Oliver?"

"I sent him the coordinates. He'll be here as soon as he can. Right now, it's just us. And Quinn." He jumped out of the SUV, and she did the same, standing beside him as he opened the hatch and released Quinn.

The Malinois sensed Justin's excitement and adrenaline. He lunged against the leash, eager to get into the woods and onto the trail. But Justin didn't release him. He didn't want Quinn giving away their presence.

Rusty knew the dogs who were part of the K-9 unit. He'd worked with Quinn on several occasions, and he'd know an alert bark if he heard it.

He'd know any bark was bad news, but hearing Quinn would set off more than alarm bells. It would send him running.

Justin wanted him to stay put, dry and cozy in the cave. Oblivious to the fact that he'd been found.

He glanced at his GPS, adjusted his trajectory, heading up a hill and through a thicket filled with brambles. Gretchen was right behind him, moving almost silently, the only sound the soft crack of branches and the quiet thud of her feet on the muddy earth.

As they walked, rain poured from the sky, falling in cold, fat drops. They slid down his head and his cheeks, pooling in the hollow of his throat and sliding under his coat and shirt. The temperature had dropped dramatically, and he wouldn't be surprised if a few snowflakes fell.

They walked three miles, crossed a creek that he remembered from one of his longer treks into the woods, and then down a steep slope.

It was quiet here. Cut off from the houses, business and traffic. Far enough away from roads to seem almost prehistoric in its beauty—thick vines hanging from old trees, rotting logs lying across sapling trees. Mushrooms and other fungi growing out of tree stumps. No hint of civilization. No trash. No broken bottles or plastic bags. The ground almost marsh-like, the air filled with the pungent scent of rotting leaves.

According to the GPS coordinates, the cave should have been a hundred yards ahead. He moved in that direction, the rain muting his footsteps and Quinn's soft whine. The dog's ears were down, his tail up, his scruff raised.

He smelled another dog.

Justin couldn't see one.

And he still couldn't see the cave.

A shadow moved to his right, and he whirled to face it, relaxing when Ava stepped into view. Roscoe was beside her, his blond fur dark with rain, his eyes bright. He looked happy to see friends, but stayed by her side, quietly moving through the foliage.

"You made it," Ava whispered as she reached Justin's side.

"Anyone else arrive?" he asked quietly.

"I'm afraid not."

"That might not be a bad thing," Gretchen said. "If the cave is big enough for him to hide in, it's big enough for firearms and explosives to be stored in. He could be well prepared to defend his position."

"*If* he's been hiding there," Ava responded. "I'm pretty certain he was carrying dog food. He had a bag over his shoulder. I couldn't get close enough to see what it was."

"This would be the perfect place to keep the dogs," Justin murmured. The area was remote enough to keep them from being heard and discovered. "Where's the cave?"

"This way." Ava led them through the woods, confident and relaxed. No sign that she'd been afraid or worried. Justin wasn't surprised. She had a reputation for being one of the best on the K-9 Search and Rescue team.

She stopped near a huge oak, standing beneath its thick limbs and pointing to the west. "There. See where the boulders are piled up?"

He did. Three large boulders, sitting against the face of a small hill. "Yes, but I don't see a cave."

"It's behind the boulders. Which is probably why none of us has ever been in it. This place isn't exactly easily accessible."

"No, but it sure does make a great place to keep something you don't want anyone to find," Gretchen said quietly, taking a step forward.

"You two stay back," Justin told them. "Quinn and I are going to take a look."

"I'm not sure that's the best idea, Captain," Ava said. "It might be better to call for some tear gas. I'd rather have him come to us than go to him when we have no idea what's he's got in there."

"I'd consider that if I were certain he didn't have any of our missing K-9s in there."

"Justin," Gretchen said, grabbing his wrist.

"I agree with Ava. It's too dangerous. You have no field of vision. No way of knowing how many people might be in that cave."

"I have Quinn," he reminded her. "He'll be my eyes and ears."

"I'll go with you, then. There's strength in numbers."

"Any other time, I'd agree," he said, "but we don't know if he's meeting someone here. We don't know if Olio has operatives heading in this direction, and we don't know if Boyd is around. I want you to stay here and stop anyone who tries to enter the cave after I go in."

"Justin—" she began, but he cut off her argument.

"We're moving ahead with my plan. Stay here. If I need help, you'll know it." He unhooked Quinn's leash and gave him the command to heel. They moved side by side, stepping between ancient pines and younger oaks. Visibility was limited in the rain and dusk, and he was glad. If he was having difficulty seeing what he knew was there, Rusty would have trouble seeing something he wasn't expecting.

And Rusty had no reason to expect someone to be approaching.

Not unless he was meeting someone.

And, even then, he wouldn't have reason to be standing watch.

Justin approached the cave cautiously, keeping to the tree line until he had a clear view of the boulders. As Ava had said, there was no visual of the cave beyond. It really was the perfect place to hide something or someone. If the team's theory was correct, Rusty had sold Patriot to the Olio Crime Syndicate. If the other dogs were in the cave, he'd either had second thoughts or he'd been bargaining for more money.

Justin had a feeling the latter was unlikely. Rusty was a good K-9 trainer but hadn't had a commanding enough personality to move quickly up through the ranks. It was doubtful he'd want to bargain with a syndicate that might decide they'd had enough and kill him.

On the other hand, Rusty had always seemed to care about the dogs. He'd spoken highly of the German shepherds who were missing, and he'd seemed legitimately upset about the trainers who'd been killed. It seemed more likely he'd seen the freed dogs as an opportunity to make some extra money and had then come to regret the deal and had brought the dogs to the cave while he tried to figure out how to rectify his mistake.

As far as Justin was concerned, there was no time like the present to find out the truth. He reached the boulders, Quinn heeling so closely they were almost touching. This was how they worked when they were moving through enemy territory. Pressed together and ready to defend one another.

Light danced on the ground to the left of the boulders. A high-powered lantern rather than fire. The air was chilly and damp, filled with the scent of rain and wet earth. Not a hint of smoke.

A dog barked, the sound muted but clearly audible.

Not Roscoe. The sound had come from the other side of the boulder. If Justin hadn't been so close to the cave, he'd have radioed Gretchen to tell her that they might have located the dogs.

Quinn growled, his hackles raised, his muscles tense.

Down, Justin signaled, and the dog immediately dropped to his stomach.

Crawl, Justin signaled again, and Quinn inched along on his stomach until they reached the edge of the boulder.

This was it. They had to breach the cave,

and they had to do it before Rusty and anyone he might be with could react.

Justin pulled his firearm, met Quinn's eyes. The dog was staring at him. Eager. Ready.

One quick signal, and the dog was off, bounding into the cave, teeth bared and growling.

Justin ran in behind him, keeping low and close to the rock face, the sound of a man's scream filling his ears.

Someone was screaming. A man.

Gretchen could hear him over the sound of Quinn's growls and barks. Not Justin. It had to be Rusty. She didn't hesitate. She didn't think it through. She knew when it was time to hold back, and she knew when it was time to move in.

"Stay here." She tossed the words at Ava as she sprinted to the boulders, rounded them and found the cave. It was deep, but well lit by a lantern. She stopped short when she saw the scene before her.

Justin kneeling over Rusty Morton, hiking his arms up behind his back and slapping on cuffs. Quinn right beside them, growling, his jaws snapping. Bags of dog food on the ground, one of them spilling kibble across the dirt. Food and water dishes. And three large German shepherds chained to stakes that had been hammered into the ground.

"Do you need help, Captain?" she asked, moving toward him, her focus on Rusty.

The trainer wasn't even trying to fight. He lay with his cheek pressed to the ground, his body lax. It seemed almost as if he were glad to have finally been found.

"No. I'm good." Justin pulled Rusty to his feet. "Good to see you again, Rusty. We've been worried about you," he remarked, pushing him into a chair.

"Worried about the dogs, you mean," Rusty said quietly. He looked…broken. His head down, his hair disheveled.

"We've been worried about you, too. It isn't like you to be AWOL. Want to tell me what's going on?" Justin asked calmly.

"I made a mistake. I was trying to fix it."

"By keeping these dogs in a cave?" Justin asked.

"By not selling them to Olio."

"So, you *were* responsible for Patriot being used by the crime organization," Gretchen said, and Rusty finally looked up. He met her eyes, and she didn't see any anger or hatred in his gaze. Just remorse.

"Yes, and I regretted it almost immediately. I love these dogs. I just wasn't thinking clearly. An Olio operative had been contacting me for months, offering me major dollars to grab one of the dogs and hand it over. When I realized someone had freed the dogs, it seemed like a perfect opportunity to get some extra cash." He swallowed hard, his skin pale and pasty, his eyes shadowed.

"And you brought them here?" Justin prodded.

"No. I put them in my van and drove off base. A friend of mine was looking after them while I worked out the details of their sale. He lives out in the country but has a nice fenced yard and experience with dogs. I went and checked on them every few days." He shrugged.

"Does your friend happen to work for Olio?" Justin asked.

Rusty hesitated.

"You may as well tell us," Gretchen said. "Eventually, it's all going to come out, and it'll be better for you if we don't have to work too hard to make that happen."

"Yes. We grew up next door to each other, and we've been friends for years. He knows what I do on base, and he was the one who suggested to the crime ring that military dogs would be perfect guards for drug and illegal weapon caches."

"So, he's your contact with Olio?" Justin asked.

"Yes. When I changed my mind about selling the rest of the dogs, I went out to his place and got the dogs who were still there. Patriot had already been sold. Olio's head honcho wanted to see how effective he was before he paid for the other dogs."

"That worked out well for you," Justin said. "It would have been difficult to get them back to base if they were already in Olio's hands."

"I know, and I can't tell you how much I regret what I did, but it wasn't criminal. It *wasn't.* I found a few stray dogs and I sold them. There's no crime in that."

"You knew they belonged to the US Air Force," Gretchen said, scratching the muzzle of the closest German shepherd. He was large and handsome, his eyes bright and alert. He'd obviously been well taken care of.

"I made a mistake. That doesn't make me a criminal, and it doesn't mean I should go to jail."

"I think the court will have something to say about that," FBI Special Agent Oliver Davison said as he walked into the cave, Ava right behind him with Roscoe.

"I can't believe it," Ava breathed, hurrying across the room and looking at the shepherds. "They're here. All of them."

"We'll have to check the microchips to be sure of that," Justin said. "But it does look like these are the missing shepherds."

He crouched near the one Gretchen was petting. "This is Scout. I'd know him anywhere."

The dog licked his cheek, and Gretchen smiled. "I guess he knows you, too."

"We do go way back, don't we, buddy?" He scratched the dog behind his ears and stood. "Gretchen, can you radio Dispatch? Have someone let Westley know that we have the dogs. He may want to come in and help transport them out. Or he can meet us back at the kennel."

"Sure." After she'd done so, she walked deeper into the cave. She could hear Oliver interrogating Rusty and the trainer giving up his friend's name and contact information.

But that wasn't all she wanted to hear. She felt a sense of failure, of frustration because there was still a loose thread that needed to be tied.

"You okay?" Justin asked, falling into step

beside her. Quinn was lying on the ground, staring at Rusty as if he'd like to make a meal of him. He didn't seem aware of the other dogs, although she was certain he'd noticed them. His focus was on the cuffed man, and she knew he'd continue to watch Rusty until he was told to back off.

"I'm fine. I'm just wondering what else Rusty is hiding in here."

"Drugs, you mean? Firearms? Because I believe his story. I think he took an opportunity and regretted it. I don't think he has anything to do with Olio's criminal operations."

"I agree. I was thinking more along the lines of roses or notes. Something that the Red Rose Killer uses." She purposely said it loud enough for Rusty to hear. The team had been leaning toward him being an opportunistic criminal, but it was still possible he'd been in league with Boyd Sullivan. The cave would certainly make a great hiding place for the serial killer.

"I had nothing to do with Boyd Sullivan's crime spree," he yelled, jumping to his feet.

Quinn growled in response, the sound terrifying enough to send a chill up Gretchen's spine.

"Really?" she asked as he dropped back into

his seat, his focus on the dog. "Because you benefited a lot from his crimes. How much were you paid for Patriot? A couple thousand dollars?"

"Ten thousand," he muttered. "But I would never hurt anyone."

"You hurt the team when you took those dogs," she said.

"I would never physically hurt someone," he corrected. "I didn't even have it in me to steal a dog. I waited until they were already loose, and then I grabbed them, because I figured a few dogs missing out of hundreds wasn't going to be a big deal."

"You were wrong about that," Ava said, scratching Roscoe behind his floppy ears. "Our dogs are family. I thought you understood that."

"I did. I *do*. But I had gambling debts to pay." He swallowed hard. "I realized as soon as I made the deal that I shouldn't have. That's why I brought these dogs here last month. I was trying to figure out a way to get them back to the kennel without having them traced to me."

"You should have asked for help," Justin said. "There isn't a person on the K-9 team who wouldn't have been willing to give it."

"I'm sorry. I really am."

Gretchen didn't want to, but she believed him.

As disappointing as it was, they'd found the missing dogs, but they were no closer to finding the Red Rose Killer.

She ran a hand over her damp hair. He should have been caught months ago. Canyon Air Force Base had one of the best Security Forces in the nation. The K-9 team was top tier. The men and women who worked there were driven by the need for justice.

And God was on their side, right?

Surely, He wanted Sullivan caught as much as they did.

So, why the wait?

Why the months of chasing leads and hitting dead ends, of trying desperately to stop a killer, only to find another victim?

There'd been too many lives lost.

Too many people hurt.

But God was good. He was love. He was righteousness.

And yet evil still existed in the world.

She strode to the mouth of the cave and stepped outside, desperate for fresh air. She let the rain fall down her cheeks like tears.

When your job meant constantly looking

for criminals, sometimes it was hard to see the good in the world. Sometimes, it was difficult to see God's work going on around you.

She acknowledged that and her own jaded viewpoint.

There were plenty of people who walked through life without ever coming up against someone like Boyd Sullivan. There were wonderful things happening every day. Even during the most difficult trials, joy could be found.

She and Henry had shared a lot of sweet and funny moments during his cancer treatment, and if he'd lived, he'd probably say the tough times had strengthened his faith. He'd been the kind of person who'd focused on the positive, and she wanted to be like that, too. Not just to honor his memory, but to honor God.

No matter what, she believed He was there, and that the way she moved through the world would lead people toward Him or away.

She walked past the boulders and away from the lantern light. In the distance, a dog barked. The K-9 trainers and their dogs must be on the way. Probably with extra hands to help bring the German shepherds out of the woods.

It would be good to have them back where they belonged.

Even with Boyd still free, the returned dogs

would raise morale and give the team something to celebrate.

She'd focus on that and on doing everything she could to make sure they found Boyd before he struck again.

"Are you okay?" Justin asked, walking around the bolder and heading toward her. His hair was glossy with rain, his expression hidden by the darkness.

"I just needed some air."

"You were hoping we'd find Boyd here."

"Weren't you?"

"Yes, but not finding him isn't the end of the road. Eventually, he'll make a mistake, and we'll be there when he does."

"Hopefully, he'll do it before someone else is hurt."

"It's unlikely anyone will. He's after me, Gretchen. He's made that very clear."

"That's what I'm worried about."

For a moment, he was silent. Then he tucked a strand of hair behind her ear, his fingers lingering against her skin. His eyes gleamed in the darkness, the softness in them making her throat tight.

"What?" she said, stepping back because she was afraid she might step forward. Into his space. Into his arms.

"You're worried about me," he said, and she could hear the smile in his voice.

"Of course I am, and it's not funny."

"I'm not laughing."

"You're amused," she accused.

"I'm…touched."

"Don't be. I'm always concerned about the people I work with." She just happened to be a little more…invested in Justin.

They'd worked countless hours together.

They'd shared stories and told jokes and treated each other to coffee when the days were long. They'd made wedding favors, and she'd looked in his eyes, and she'd felt things she hadn't felt in years. Hope. Excitement. Attraction.

"You don't have to worry, Gretchen. I'm not planning on letting Boyd win," he said.

"It's not your plans I'm worried about. It's Boyd's. Maybe even God's. It's not like we know what He has in store."

"'All things work together for good to them that love God,'" he replied. "Corbin used to quote that all the time. I can't remember the chapter and verse, but it seems appropriate to the situation."

"It's easy to quote Scripture. It's not always easy to believe the words."

"I know." He put his hands on her shoulders, and she could feel the weight of his palms, the strength of his fingers. She could feel his warmth seeping through her soaked jacket, and for a moment, she felt like she'd finally found that sweet place called home. The one she missed so much when she was away from her family. The one she'd felt like she'd lost when Henry died.

She would have stepped away, but he was studying her face, his eyes gleaming in the darkness, and she wasn't sure what he was looking for, wasn't sure if she wanted him to find it.

"We've both been hurt, we've both lost, we've both struggled to hold on to our faith," he said as if he'd read that in her face. As if, somehow, he had looked in her eyes and seen all the questions and worries she hid from the world. "And we're both standing here, knowing we might just have found something we weren't even looking for. That's a scary thing. Don't think I don't know it and feel it. Don't think I'm not just as worried about it as you are."

"We were talking about Boyd," she pointed out, her voice raspy with emotion. She'd always been a straight shooter, quick to speak her mind. Right now, though, she couldn't make herself agree. Even though everything he'd said was true.

"We were also talking about faith and God's plan. The way I see things, it all ties together." He wiped rain from her cheeks, and she could see his smile through the darkness. "So, how about we spend less time worrying and more time trusting that things will be okay?"

She nodded, because she was afraid to speak. Afraid that the emotion in her voice would give away all her fear and anxiety and hope and excitement.

"Good," he said, leaning down so that they were eye to eye. She could feel his breath fanning her face, see the tenderness in his expression.

When he kissed her, it felt right. Like sunrise after the darkest night. Like the first rays of light after a storm.

When he broke away, she was breathless, her hands clutching his arms.

"Justin—" she began.

"Let's not ruin the moment by overthinking it, okay?" he said gently.

"I just don't want to have my heart broken again," she admitted.

"I would never break your heart," he promised.

"Henry didn't plan to, either," she said, her voice raw and hot with emotion.

A quiet click broke through the sound of rain splattering on leaves and splashing on the ground.

Gretchen recognized it immediately. Pulling her gun from the holster, she swung in the direction of the sound.

She didn't have a chance to fire.

Justin was on her, tackling her to the ground as he fired into the trees.

TEN

Justin was on his feet before the sound of gunfire faded to silence, pulling Gretchen to her feet, asking if she was okay. Listening to the crash of someone fleeing through the woods.

Not someone.

Boyd. He knew that the same way he knew that the click of the safety being released was another game. Sullivan might have been average in basic training, but he'd been an ace at target practice. If he'd been willing to do the work, he'd have made an excellent sharpshooter. Even if his skills were rusty, he'd have been able to hit a target.

It wasn't like Justin and Gretchen had been on the move. They'd been sitting ducks, waiting for the bullets to fly.

But Boyd hadn't taken the shot.

He probably had a list of offenses that had been committed against him, and he wanted to explain every one of them before he ended things. He wouldn't be happy to kill someone from a distance. He wanted to take the shot close-up. He fed off the fear of others.

Justin fed off locking people like him away.

"That was close," Gretchen said, straightening her pack. Her voice was shaky, but he didn't think that was because of Boyd.

The kiss had upset her.

Because she didn't want her heart broken again.

That was what she'd said, and he'd planned to ask if she were willing to risk it, anyway. Now wasn't the time, though. Boyd was on the move, and he planned to go after him.

"Not as close as he'd have liked," he replied, unhooking Quinn's leash. The dog lunged toward the woods, straining against the hold Justin had on his collar.

"Is everyone okay?" Oliver called, rushing out of the cave, Ava and Roscoe behind him.

"Fine. Quinn and I are going after him." Justin released the collar, snapping the command that freed Quinn to do what he did best.

The dog took off, racing into the woods, barking wildly.

More dogs took up the cry. The team was closing in, and he'd have plenty of backup if he needed it, but Justin wasn't going to wait around to give instructions. He set off into the woods.

"Can you see Quinn?" Gretchen asked as she ran up beside him.

"No, but I don't need to. I've already given him his command. He knows what to do."

"What if he finds Boyd and is hurt?" she asked.

"That's the risk I take every time I release him to apprehend a criminal."

"I'm not sure I could do it," she admitted. "I'd worry too much."

"Then you're better off doing the kind of work Ava does. Search and rescue is dangerous. But not like this."

"Does it ever get to you? Or are you really as unaffected as you seem?"

"It gets to me all the time. I've had Quinn for three years. I got him straight out of his K-9 training. He's family. I'd give my life to save his, but this is his job, Gretchen. He loves it. So I tell myself that it's no different than you or me walking into a dangerous situation. We're well trained. If something happens, it won't be because of anything we did wrong."

"At least, we hope not," she said, panting slightly as they crested a hill.

Lights flashed in the distance. One. Then another and another.

It took a moment for him to realize he was looking at cars.

A road.

Boyd's escape route.

He radioed the team, asking for the road to be ID'd and MPs to be dispatched to the area. They needed to set up blockades to keep Boyd from fleeing in a vehicle.

If they could keep him on foot, their chances of capturing him were better.

Up ahead, Quinn was bounding down the hill, his body a black blur in the darkness. He wasn't barking. Wasn't growling. Which meant he was closing in on his prey.

Justin raced after him, feet sliding on muddy ground and wet leaves, heart racing. The road was close. He could hear cars speeding past, but the trees were thicker near the bottom of the hill, the brambles catching at his clothes.

He finally broke through thick undergrowth, stumbling onto the breakdown lane of a four-lane highway.

"Is this the interstate?" Gretchen asked, still right on his heels and keeping pace.

"It's a state highway. Unless I've gotten

turned around, the north entrance to the base is a few miles to the right."

"Quinn is heading in the opposite direction," she pointed out.

"Then Boyd must be, too." He took off, running full-speed down the road, Quinn a swiftly moving shadow in front of him.

They rounded a bend, and he saw a small sedan idling on the side of the road. He saw Boyd next, his blond hair nearly white in the streetlight, his long legs eating up the ground.

He glanced over his shoulder, probably trying to see how close Quinn was.

"Police! Stop and keep your hands where I can see them," Justin called, but Boyd had reached the vehicle, was yanking open the passenger door and jumping inside.

Quinn reached the car seconds later, jumping up against the window and door, snarling and snapping.

"Off!" Justin called, afraid Boyd would shoot through the window.

Quinn backed off reluctantly, his attention on the car.

"Heel!" Justin yelled as the engine revved and the vehicle jumped forward.

Quinn spun away, racing back to Justin and pressing close to his left leg. They moved in tandem, sprinting after the car. Sirens screamed in the background.

Justin wanted to pull his gun and take a shot, but there were cars filled with civilians passing by, and he couldn't risk injury to one of them.

When the taillights of the sedan disappeared, Justin finally stopped running.

Disappointed.

Frustrated.

Angry that he hadn't been just a little faster.

He'd been minutes away from capturing Boyd, and once again, the killer had slipped through his fingers.

"I got a partial plate," Gretchen said, panting as she pulled out her phone and typed something into it. "Were you able to get the make or model of the car?"

"It was a Toyota. I'm not sure what model. Four-door. Black or dark blue. That's about all I saw."

"How about the driver?"

"Nothing. The interior lights were off."

"Too bad."

"Why do you say that?"

"I think it's someone from the base. Someone we know. We need to contact gate security and ask them to keep an eye out for the car.

Did you use the secure radio frequency when you called headquarters?"

"Yes." And that meant only Security Forces officers and dispatchers had access to the communication. As much as he hated to admit it, Gretchen was right.

"Make the call," he said. "I'm going to talk to the MPs who are arriving." He gestured toward a cruiser that was speeding toward them, lights flashing, sirens blaring.

She nodded, already speaking into the radio. From running in the rain, her hair was hanging across her cheeks, thick wet strands clinging to silky skin.

He was tempted to brush it away, but the cruiser had parked, and two officers were getting out. They'd see any gesture he made toward her. He didn't care, but he knew Gretchen would.

So he walked away, Quinn still on heel beside him. The fact that Gretchen had gotten a partial plate impressed him, but he wasn't sure it would bring them any closer to Boyd. The killer had a predilection for stealing cars and using them when he was on the prowl. More than likely, the Toyota had been stolen.

That didn't mean that the person driving it wasn't military personnel. Gretchen's assessment had been spot-on. Someone with inside information was helping Boyd.

Justin's mission was to find out who.

It was 3:00 a.m. when Gretchen finally finished writing up her report, shut down her computer and grabbed her backpack from the floor beside her chair. She and Justin had been back at the office for several hours, going over lists of possible leaks, attempting to obtain phone records for everyone who'd been working in the building when Justin made radio contact.

That would take time.

Until Gretchen had them in hand, she'd have no idea who had made the call that had sent Boyd to the cave.

She lifted her coffee, sipping the last dregs of her fifth cup.

Or was it her sixth?

She should have been wired from the caffeine. All she felt was bone-deep fatigue.

"All set?" Justin asked, pushing away from his desk and standing. They'd been alone in the office for at least an hour, the quiet hum of their computers muffling the sound of people walking through the hallway outside. She'd done her best to ignore him, but her thoughts seemed to constantly move in his direction. She'd wanted to talk to him rather than work in silence, but the things she'd had to say had nothing to do with the case and everything to do with the kiss.

If she let herself, she could still feel the warmth of his lips against hers.

Her cheeks heated, and she stood. "Yes. Finally."

She sounded normal, she thought. She *hoped.*

"Quinn and I will take you home." He grabbed her coat from the back of the chair and draped it around her shoulders.

"That's not necessary, Justin. I can walk from here."

"I'd rather you not. Boyd was watching us tonight."

"So?" She brushed a crumb from her desk, moved her pen so that it was neatly centered on the computer keyboard. Anything to avoid meeting his eyes.

She was falling for him.

Hard.

And she didn't want him to see the truth of that in her eyes. She was too afraid of what it would mean, too afraid to commit herself to tumbling headfirst into something new and exciting and terrifying.

"So, he might have seen me do this." He tucked a strand of hair behind her ear, his fingers drifting from her cheek to her ear, and then down to the column of her throat.

"I don't remember you doing that," she murmured, but she didn't move away. She *should* have. Of course she should have.

Because she didn't want a repeat of the kiss.

She *didn't*.

"Okay, so maybe it was more like this." He shifted his hands so that they rested on her shoulders, and she found herself moving closer. Not because he asked or demanded it. Because she couldn't seem to stop herself.

This time, his kiss was as gentle as a warm spring breeze. Soft and tender and filled with promise of things to come.

"Either way," he murmured as he pulled back, "Boyd may have seen it, and he may have decided you're the perfect way to get to me."

"The only way he could use me like that is to kidnap me," she managed to say.

"That's my point. Let's not make you an easy target, okay? I'll take you home. You'll lock the door, and you won't unlock it until you call and let me know you need an escort."

His thumb brushed the pulse point in her neck, the raspy slide of it sending heat up her spine.

"You can't escort me everywhere I need to go," she protested.

"If I can't, I'll send someone else. Just until this is over." He studied her face, his gaze intense and unwavering. "You don't have to be scared, Gretchen."

"I'm not scared. I'm terrified."

"Of Boyd?"

"Of my stupid fickle heart," she blurted out, and he smiled.

"I'm serious, Justin," she muttered. "My heart has already been broken once. I don't think I'll survive it a second time around."

"Who's to say there will be a second time? Maybe your heart will be just fine."

"This is a dangerous job. Either of us could get injured." Or worse. She didn't add that.

He knew what she was thinking.

No one got into a relationship with a law enforcement officer without understanding the risk.

"That's true, but I'd rather give my all to something and have my heart broken than sit in a safe little bubble and never experience life," he responded.

"That's interesting. Coming from you."

"What's that supposed to mean?"

"You're in your thirties and still single. Obviously, you're not all that eager to take relationship risks."

"Me being single has nothing to do avoiding risks. At least, not in the way you're thinking."

"Then what does it have to do with?" she asked, genuinely curious. Justin was a great guy. He had a good career that earned him good money. If he stayed in the military until retirement, he'd have a good pension. He was handsome, smart and funny. Any woman would consider herself fortunate to be with a man like him.

"The truth?" he asked.

"I certainly prefer it to a lie."

"I'm single because the only example of a husband and father I had was my dad. He beat my mother for fun, and he did the same to me."

His words were like ice water, cooling her blood, clearing her head.

"I'm sorry, Justin. That's horrible," she said.

"It was, but watching him taught me what being a man wasn't. Now I'm doing everything I can to be what he wasn't. I'm not afraid of having my heart broken. I'm afraid of breaking the heart of someone I love. I'm afraid of turning into a selfish, angry monster who only cares about his own needs and desires." He paused, a frown line between his brows. "Or I *was* afraid of those things. Portia has been with me for over a year, and I haven't flown off the handle yet. I'm hoping that's a good sign."

"You don't need a sign. If you were like your father, you wouldn't be able to do this job. Being the head of Security Forces requires self-control and patience. If you didn't have those things, you'd be sunk."

"Maybe you're right. I hope you're right." His gaze dropped to her lips, and her breath caught. She was pretty sure her heart stopped, too.

"You can tell me to stop, if you want me to," he said, leaning down until they were just a hairbreadth away.

She knew she should.

She knew she was setting herself up for heartbreak, but she couldn't make herself say the words.

His lips brushed hers. Just like they had before. Gently. Tenderly.

Tears burned behind her eyes, and she pulled away, breathless, off balance.

"We shouldn't be doing this," she said, her heart still pounding wildly.

"Why not? There's no rule against it."

"It's not about rules. It's about me going back to Minot in a few weeks. It's about you staying here. It's about long-distance relationships not working."

"Your brother is in Texas. Your future sister-in-law is in New England," he pointed out.

"They're an exception."

"We can be an exception, too. If we want to be." He took a step away, watching her, waiting for a response.

But everything she thought of saying seemed trite and dishonest. Nothing seemed to match up to the magnitude of this moment and this conversation, because no amount of fear seemed insurmountable when she looked into his eyes.

She was going to tell him that.

She *was*, but the door opened, and Oliver walked into the room.

He glanced at Gretchen and then at Justin.

"Sorry," he said, starting to close the door again.

"It's okay. What's up?" Justin walked toward him, his posture stiff, his expression unreadable.

She'd hurt him.

She knew she had.

And she wanted to take it all back, tell him

that she'd been stupid. That, of course, she was willing to risk her heart again. For him.

"My transport to Houston will be here shortly," Oliver said. "Rusty is already cooperating. He's given us a few names and the address of a storage unit that he thinks Patriot was guarding. He believes Olio was keeping drugs or weapons in it."

"If you find it, you may find the person who owns it," Justin said.

"Right, and we're hoping that person can give us names. We're getting close to closing the crime ring down, and I wanted to thank you both for your help."

"Thank us when Olio no longer exists," Justin said. "Until then, let me know if you need any more help."

"Thanks. I'll also keep you updated. And before I forget..." He pulled a folded piece of paper from his pocket and handed it to Justin. "Portia gave this to one of my men and asked if we could deliver it to you. I'd planned to give it to you earlier, but things got a little crazy."

"That's an understatement."

"See you later." Oliver hurried away, and Justin unfolded the note, smiling as he read it.

"Is she doing okay?" Gretchen asked.

"Yes." He folded the note again, tucked it into his pocket without sharing any of the details.

He was putting up barriers.

That was clear, and she couldn't even be upset, because she was the one who'd demanded them.

"Justin," she began, determined to clear the air. To explain. To apologize.

"How about we discuss it later?"

"You don't even know what I was going to say."

"I know that I need to get you home. It's been a long day. We're both tired, and I have a team meeting scheduled for ten. If you're not up to attending, I'll understand, but I have to be there. I'd like to get some sleep before then."

"Since when have I ever missed a meeting?"

"I'm just giving you the option. Not implying that you'll choose it." He called to Quinn and walked out of the room.

She followed, knowing she'd made a mistake. Knowing she was the only one who could fix it. She'd have pulled Justin to a stop and forced him to hear her out, but now didn't seem like the time.

Like he'd said, it had been a long day. They were both tired.

Tomorrow would be soon enough to explain herself.

They made the drive back to her place in silence.

Justin left Quinn in the SUV and walked her to her apartment. He waited as she unlocked the door. Just like he had dozens of times before.

Only this time felt like the last time.

This time felt like the end.

She reached for his hand, but his phone rang before she could touch him.

He answered, his voice rumbling through the hallway, the words terse and a little sharp. "You're sure? Okay. I'll swing by on my way home. See if I find anything."

"What's going on?" she asked as he tucked the phone back in his pocket.

"That was the desk sergeant. An airman called. She was on her way back from furlough and thought she saw a red rose lying on the sidewalk in front of the high school."

"Another message from Boyd?"

"Maybe. Although I don't know why he'd leave it there when Portia is out of his reach."

"Maybe he wants you to panic and contact her?"

"He's not going to get what he wants. I never panic. But I will go check it out."

"I'll come with you."

"Not this time. I have Quinn, and I don't think I'm going to find anything. It's dark and rainy. Sticks look like swords in weather like this. A clump of grass might look like a rose."

She didn't argue.

He was probably right. The likelihood of Boyd leaving a rose on the sidewalk was slim.

"All right. I'll see you in the morning," she said, stepping into the apartment and closing the door.

She turned the lock and flicked on the light.

Only, the room remained dark.

Surprised, she walked across the living room and switched on the lamp. Like the overhead light, it didn't go on.

She planned to walk into the hall that led to the bedrooms and try the light there. If it didn't work, she'd call management and ask if a circuit had blown. She stepped toward the hall and stopped.

This wasn't right.

None of it.

The light in the hall outside the apartment had been on.

The last time a circuit had blown, it had been out.

This made no sense... Unless someone had

entered her apartment and removed light bulbs or cut lines.

She went cold at the thought, her skin crawling as she walked to the door. She told herself not to run, because if someone was in the apartment, she didn't want him to know she suspected it.

Someone?

Boyd. If Boyd were in the apartment…

"Please, God," she whispered.

"I don't think He hears you," a deep voice responded.

She whirled around, ready to fight.

Pain exploded through her head, and she fell into nothingness.

ELEVEN

There'd been no red rose. He'd spent an hour searching the sidewalks near the school, and he'd come up empty. When Justin tried to find the airman who'd called in the report, he couldn't. She hadn't given her name, hadn't offered an address, and the phone number she'd called from was unlisted. He suspected the phone was prepaid and impossible to trace.

Thinking about that had kept him from sleeping.

No sleep led to a bad mood that no amount of cafeteria coffee seemed able to ease. He dumped a packet of sugar into his cup and took a sip.

That wasn't doing it for him, either.

Not that his mood would have been stellar if he'd gotten a full eight hours. He'd made a jerk of himself with Gretchen last night, taking offense because she hadn't been willing to step out in faith with him. He could blame that on fatigue as well, but he didn't make a habit of lying to himself.

Over the past few months, he and Gretchen had built a rapport and a relationship, and he'd been intrigued enough to want to try for more. After spending the afternoon with her, he'd thought she'd felt the same. They'd clicked, fitted together like two halves of a whole, and it had felt as right to him as sunrise in the morning or snow in the winter.

She obviously hadn't felt the same.

If she had, she'd have been more willing to let go of the past and step into the future. Whatever it brought.

At least, that was how he'd felt last night.

In the cold hard light of day, he wasn't as convinced.

He set his coffee on the conference room table and glanced at the clock. Ten o'clock, and, as if on cue, the door opened and Westley and Felicity walked in. They both looked tired but happy.

"Good morning," Felicity said cheerfully, grabbing a mug and pouring coffee for herself and Westley. "Any news from Oliver? I was hoping that a miracle occurred, and the

FBI located the Olio kingpin. The crime ring needs to go down for what it did to our dogs."

"Were they injured?" he asked, eager for a report from Westley now that he'd had a chance to get the three German shepherds examined by the base vet.

"No, but they're traumatized. It's going to take some time for them to get acclimated." Westley pulled a chair out for Felicity and then took a seat, his dog, Dakota, settling down beside him.

"Fortunately, we can give them that," Felicity said, glancing around the room and frowning.

"What's wrong?" he asked.

"Where's Yvette?"

"She's not here?" Ava stepped into the room, Roscoe loping beside her. If she was tired from the late night, it didn't show.

"Maybe she didn't realize we were meeting?" Justin offered.

It *was* strange.

Since Boyd had been on the loose, she'd been at every meeting regarding the Red Rose Killer. The fact that she'd received a rose from him had made her a part of the group.

"How's everyone?" Vanessa Gomez asked as she walked into the room. A nurse who worked at the base hospital, she'd nearly been killed by a Red Rose Killer copycat. She'd become involved in the quest to stop Boyd when she'd thought she was his target. Even after she'd learned the truth, she'd remained part of the team. Tech Sergeant Linc Colson was right behind her with Nick Donovan. Oliver was back in Houston working on the Olio ring, so everyone on the team was accounted for.

Except one.

Gretchen hadn't arrived.

He glanced at the clock again—10:10 a.m. Not exceptionally late, but Gretchen was always early. His mood took a nosedive, the rose and the airman who'd reported it nagging at the back of his mind. He should have stopped by her apartment and offered her a ride. He had told her not to leave the house without an escort, but he'd been preparing for the meeting and time had gotten away from him.

And he'd assumed she'd call.

That she'd realize the seriousness of the situation and agree to his plan.

"Is Gretchen coming?" Linc asked, his attention on the empty seat.

"She was really tired last night. We've had a couple of long days," he hedged.

"Want me to call her?" Vanessa asked, pulling out her cell phone.

"I told her she could skip if she wanted to," Justin admitted, and the team went silent. No more quiet conversation. No more rustling papers as they looked through the case notes he'd put together for them.

"You told her she didn't have to attend?" Nick asked. "Why?"

"I already explained that," he replied, glancing at the clock again. Fifteen minutes after the meeting was supposed to begin, and she still wasn't there. And if he knew anything about Gretchen, it was that she didn't skip meetings and she never shirked responsibility.

She should be there.

She wasn't, and the team was right to be concerned.

"But you're right. It's not like her to not show." He pulled out his cell phone and called, waiting impatiently for her to pick up.

She didn't, and the unsettled feeling in his gut intensified.

"She's not home?" Ava asked.

Like Justin, the team knew Gretchen's work ethic.

"Not answering," he corrected.

"Who's not answering?" Oliver walked into

the room, crossing to Ava and setting his hands on his fiancée's shoulders.

"Gretchen," she responded, looking up to meet his eyes. "What are you doing here? I thought you were staying in Houston."

"Just until we got the information we needed. And we did. We picked up Rusty's friend last night. He's singing like a canary. We got several names and addresses. We also went to a storage unit he told us about. We found all the equipment needed to counterfeit currency. We put out an arrest warrant for the owner of the property, brought him in and got a list of names. We have a dozen people in custody."

"That's wonderful!" Ava said.

It was. If the FBI hadn't completely shut down Olio, they'd put a huge dent in its operations. Even if it managed to limp along for a while longer, it wouldn't survive.

"So, what's going on with Gretchen?" Oliver asked, taking the empty seat.

"She's not here," Ava responded. "Which isn't typical. She's usually the first to arrive and the last to leave."

"I've noticed that about her." Oliver frowned. "You tried to call her?"

"Yes."

"Maybe the next step is going to her apartment. If she's there, we can have the meeting at her place."

It was a better idea than sitting around hoping she'd show up.

Justin stood, grabbing his coffee and notebook. "Quinn, heel."

He left the room, the rest of the team filing out behind him.

The apartment's parking lot was nearly empty, and Justin spotted Gretchen's car easily. Parked where it usually was. Just a few spaces away from the lobby door.

He jumped out of the SUV, not bothering to wait for the rest of the team. His heart was racing, adrenaline coursing through him, telling him something was wrong.

He released Quinn and ran into the building, bypassing the elevator and taking the stairs two at a time. He made it to the third floor in seconds, shoving open the stairwell door and running into the hall.

He realized her door was open before he reached it.

He could see a sliver of darkness beyond the well-lit hallway and his heart sank. He rapped on the door, stepping inside as it swung open.

Quinn growled deep in his throat, his shoulders hunched with tension as he lunged against his leash.

"Find," Justin commanded, releasing the dog, letting him bound through the living room. He ran down the hall and scratched at a closed door.

Justin knocked. When he got no answer, he turned the handle and walked into the room. And he saw the long-stemmed rose lying in the middle of the bed. There was a note beside it, the letters scrawled in thick black marker—*You're next.*

"He has her." He whirled around, nearly knocking Westley off his feet as he retraced his steps down the hall. Quinn was ahead of him, sniffing the floor, the walls, the couch.

"The light is out," Nick said, flicking a switch near the door.

The words barely registered. Justin couldn't think of anything else but Gretchen. If anything happened to her, he'd never forgive himself.

"This one, too," Oliver said, glancing under the lampshade, then dragging a chair into the hall and checking the light fixture there. "No bulb. Looks like someone was here ahead of her, and made sure she was in the dark."

"How about we name that someone?" Justin

said through gritted teeth. "Boyd has her. I'm taking Quinn to see if we can find their trail."

"Hold on." Nick grabbed his arm before he could leave. "I don't think running off half-cocked is going to help anything."

"It's better than standing around hoping something turns up."

His phone rang, and he grabbed it, glancing at the number.

Unknown caller.

He knew, though. Before he answered. Before he heard Boyd's voice.

"Hello," he barked, and Boyd chuckled.

"You sound cheerful this morning."

"Where is she?"

"If you're talking about your girlfriend, she's in a safe place. For now."

"Let me speak to her," he demanded, his tension making Quinn pace restlessly. The dog was feeding off his energy. If they were going to search effectively, Justin needed to dial it down.

"Sorry. I call the shots now. You want to talk to her, you'll have to find her."

"I don't like hide-and-seek."

"I do. So, you have until midnight to figure this out. If you don't. She dies." He disconnected, and Justin was tempted to toss the phone across the room. Breaking it wouldn't achieve his goal, though.

And his goal was to find Gretchen.

The team had gathered around him, everyone waiting for him to make a decision or give a command.

He took a steadying breath, forced himself to focus. "He has her, and he's playing games again. He's given me until midnight to find her."

"Did he give you any clues?" Ava asked.

"Not this time. Our best option is to take the dogs out and start searching."

"Where? On base?" Nick walked into the bedroom and grabbed the pillow, holding it out for Annie to sniff.

"Could he have gotten back on base without gate security stopping him?" Vanessa asked.

"He could have if he were in the trunk of a car that belonged to someone who had ID." Justin had taken the pillow and was holding it in front of Quinn's nose. The dog inhaled deeply, his tail wagging.

He knew Gretchen.

He liked her.

Please, God, let Quinn be able to find her.

"I know we're in a hurry, and you don't have time to waste," Vanessa said. "But I keep going back to the conference room and those snacks. A couple of months ago Gretchen and I followed Yvette, remember? We were trying to see if she was helping Boyd."

"Right," Justin said. "I remember, but she wasn't caught doing anything out of the ordinary. She's clean."

"Or she overheard the plans and made sure she didn't do anything suspicious. Think about it. Lately she's always at headquarters. Always. Every time I turn a corner it seems like she's there."

It was true. Justin had noticed the same thing. "That makes her nosy. Not guilty," he said, but he was thinking about the missing snacks, too. Thinking about the phone call last night and the report of the rose on the sidewalk in front of the high school. All of it timed just right. If Boyd had been in the apartment, he'd have heard Gretchen return. He'd have realized Justin was with her, and he could have easily hidden somewhere, called someone and had the false report made.

Yvette had dated him when they were in basic training.

She'd broken up with him, but Justin remembered the relationship—how eager she'd been to please Boyd. How callous he'd been to her.

He'd been relieved when Boyd was dishonorably discharged, and hopeful that Yvette would find someone who treated her better.

Had she contacted him while he was in prison?

Or had he reached out to her after he escaped?

If so, she'd probably been a willing pawn, eager for a relationship. She was also knowledgeable about the base. Well liked by everyone.

"You're thinking what I'm thinking," Oliver said, and Justin met his eyes.

"Yvette," he said, because he knew they were on the right track. "She'd have been able to get past gate security easily. She was at headquarters when I broke radio silence, and she probably called Boyd immediately. I gave the coordinates, so he'd have had no trouble finding the cave. She drove off base in her car, met him and they drove to the state highway together. She could easily have gotten him on base in the trunk of her car. He got into Gretchen's apartment and waited for her to return."

"Then what?" Vanessa asked. "There aren't a lot of places on base where he could hide her. Plus, transporting her wouldn't be easy. She's tall, and she knows to fight. If he managed to knock her out, he'd still have the problem of getting her out of the building without anyone noticing."

"Maybe he didn't take her out of the building," Ava said. When they all turned a questioning eye to her, she explained. "Yvette lives on the fourth floor."

"In this apartment complex?" Justin asked, his heart slamming against his ribs, his muscles tight with the need to act.

"In this building. I was there last year. She offered a healthy cooking class to people on the K-9 Search and Rescue team. She's in 418. It's on this side of the building and has a balcony that looks over the parking lot. Just like that one." She gestured toward the sliding glass door that opened out onto a small deck.

"Let's go." Westley headed for the door, but Justin grabbed his arm.

"If he hears us coming, he'll kill her for the fun of it."

"Then what's the plan?"

Good question, and Justin needed to come up with an answer. One that would keep the team safe, keep Gretchen safe and bring Boyd and Yvette to justice.

He walked to the sliding glass door but

didn't open it. If Boyd or Yvette were watching, he didn't want to give them any hint that he planned to access Yvette's apartment. It was just above Gretchen's, and should be easy enough to enter. If they were careful.

Stealth was the key, and he and Quinn were good at it. They'd ascend the fire escape and cut through the sliding glass door. He had the tool in his tactical vest. All he needed was a diversion.

"We pretend to do what we'd be doing if we didn't think Gretchen was in this building. Team up. Take the dogs out. I'll take Quinn around to the east wing of the apartment complex and go in through the service door there. The basements are connected, and I should be able to access this wing easily."

"You don't think we're going to let you do this alone, do you?" Westley said. "Because that's not going to happen. You may be the captain of the team, but we plan together and we execute together."

"You're all going to be my diversion. Create plenty of radio traffic. Make things up if you have to, but make sure it sounds like we're out searching, still trying to figure out where Gretchen's being held. Unless I miss my guess, Yvette has a scanner in her apartment. She's probably been monitoring our team for months."

"What I'm hearing you say," Oliver said, "is that you're planning to do this alone."

"Quinn and I are going to climb up the fire escape and access the balcony that way. I'll need someone to go to the front door and offer a distraction. Yvette didn't show up at the office today. That's a good enough excuse to do a well check." He glanced around at the group. "But we'll need to be careful. Boyd isn't stupid. He's going to be hard to surprise."

"Isaac can do it," Vanessa said. "I texted him and asked him to bring Beacon."

Justin nodded. Her fiancé, Isaac Goddard, was a senior airman and former fighter pilot. He'd returned from Afghanistan with PTSD and the desperate desire to bring home the German shepherd that had saved his life while he was overseas. It had taken months and a lot of red tape, but Beacon had finally been flown to the base. While Isaac was waiting, he'd saved Vanessa from an attacker and had been instrumental in stopping an air force psychiatrist who had been selling drugs on the black market and treating his patients with placebos. Justin had found Isaac to be smart, tough and quick thinking. Beacon was proving to be an excellent therapy dog for him, but Isaac wasn't content to get the therapy certification. He'd been training Beacon in obedience and protection. The shepherd was as smart as any of the dogs they had in the kennel.

"Have him text me so we can coordinate the timing," he said. "Let's move out."

They stepped out into the hall, dogs and handlers moving in sync as they walked into the stairwell. They didn't try to be quiet. Justin wanted Boyd to think he had the upper hand. That, combined with his arrogance, would be his undoing.

Justin knew what needed to be done.

He knew he and Quinn could do it.

He could only pray that they'd be able to do it quickly enough and that Gretchen wouldn't be injured during the process.

Blood still flowed sluggishly from a wound in her head, and she was pretty sure she had a concussion. Her vision was blurry, her stomach churning, but she wasn't going down without a fight.

Gretchen knew what Boyd planned. She'd heard him on the phone with Justin. He wanted to draw Justin out and kill him. Once that was accomplished, he'd kill her.

She scanned the bedroom in Yvette's apartment, looking for something that she could use to her advantage. There was a bed. A dresser. The two chairs. A bookshelf filled with books.

She shifted, trying to ease the throbbing pain in her shoulders. Boyd had handcuffed her to a high-back chair, her arms pulled through the spindles in the back. The cuffs were loose, and she could move her arms, but they were pulled so far behind her, she thought they might pop out of the sockets.

"I hope you're not trying to escape," Yvette said quietly. She was sitting in another high-back chair, staring at Gretchen as if she were afraid she'd pull a magic trick and disappear.

"How do you suppose I'm going to do that?" Gretchen asked, her head pounding with every word.

"I don't know, but the last time I watched a prisoner, he escaped. Boyd and I had a huge fight about it. We didn't speak for a month."

"Who was that?"

Yvette replied, "Why do you want to know?"

"Just curious."

"Nosiness can get a person killed," she said. "Look at you. You came here to learn some new skills, but you couldn't keep yourself from butting in where you didn't belong. Now..."

She shook her head sadly, and if Gretchen hadn't known better, she'd have thought Yvette felt bad for what was happening.

"It's my job to track down criminals, Yvette. You know that." She felt dizzy, darkness edging in, but she had to keep it together. She had to escape before Boyd accomplished his goal. If something happened to her, and Justin lived, he'd blame himself. She knew that for certain. She'd feel the same if she survived and he didn't.

They both had to come out of this alive.

Please, Lord, help me figure this out, she prayed silently.

"Boyd is not a criminal," Yvette said.

"What do you call a murderer?"

"He didn't murder anyone!" she spit. "He was forced to seek vengeance on people who were trying to destroy him. If he hadn't killed them, they'd have killed him. It was self-defense."

"Do you hear yourself, Yvette? You're defending a man who took innocent lives. Who ambushed a bodyguard and killed him because he was in the way. Who kidnapped a sixteen-year-old girl and terrorized her."

"The bodyguard shouldn't have taken the job," she said coldly. "And Portia has a big mouth. She needs to learn to keep it shut. If she hadn't been blogging and saying all those hurtful things about Boyd, he'd have left her alone."

"The bodyguard needed money to support his wife and children. He took the job because your boyfriend threatened a kid."

"He's more than my boyfriend. He's my fiancé."

"Really?" Gretchen said, purposely looking at Yvette's empty ring finger.

"He's going to get me a ring as soon as he—" She frowned.

"Kills me and Justin?" She shifted again. Between the throbbing in her shoulders and the pounding in her head, she was having difficulty focusing, but she had to pull herself together.

There was always a way out.

One of her brothers had told her that when she was a kid and he'd brought her into a carnival fun house. She'd been seven, and she'd hated it. The mirrors. The noises. The oddly moving floors. She'd been certain they were going to get trapped there.

There's always a way out.

Currently, she couldn't see one.

"Look," Yvette said, leaning forward, her

expression earnest and sweet. "You have to understand. Boyd is special. He's got a lot to give to the world. He can't do that from prison."

"So far," Gretchen responded, "he's taken more from the world than he's given. Those people who died? They were gifted, too. We all are, Yvette. Boyd isn't someone put on earth to rule us all. He's a human being. Fallible and fallen."

"He's everything to me," she retorted, sitting back and looking away. "And I'm everything to him. He says that I look like one of those Greek statues they have in the museums."

"You look like a petulant child." The words slipped out, and Yvette jumped to her feet.

"I'm going to tell Boyd to kill you now. You're mean and hateful, and all you've done is cause problems." She fled the room, and Gretchen could hear her high-pitched voice as she explained things to Boyd.

Hopefully, she had a lot to say.

Gretchen's tactical vest had been removed, and she could see it lying in the corner of the room. Her gun was gone, and she was pretty certain that was the weapon Boyd planned to murder her with.

He'd like the irony of that and the power it made him feel.

She tugged at the cuffs, knowing she'd never get her hands through them, but she felt compelled to try. She shoved her feet under the chair, trying to stand. If she could, maybe she could make it to the vest. She wasn't sure what she could do with it while her hands were cuffed behind her back, but at least she'd have more options.

"Going somewhere?" Boyd asked, stepping into the room, Gretchen's service weapon in his hand.

She was cold with fear, but she wasn't going to let him know it. "Trying to stretch my legs. I'm not used to sitting for ten hours."

"It hasn't been that long," he said, stopping beside her and pressing the barrel of the gun to her head.

She was helpless, and he knew it.

She was terrified, and he probably knew that, too.

But she planned to decide how she'd die. Cowering wasn't it.

"Does killing people who can't fight back make you feel like a man?" she said, moving her feet, trying to widen her stance so she could get enough leverage to throw herself sideways and knock him over.

"I'm not going to lose my cool because you

taunt me. If you're hoping to make me lose my concentration, you're going to be disappointed."

"I have a feeling you lose your cool all the time. Bullies usually do."

"She wants me to kill you. You know that, right?" He flicked her hair with the gun, scowling when she didn't wince.

"I'm not surprised. I figured she was the one calling the shots. I've heard about your time in basic training. Your work was mediocre at best. If you'd graduated, you'd have been at the bottom of the class. Yvette was better. I think she was in the top ten percent. It's not surprising that she's the one who's planned this all out."

"I do the planning," he growled. "And I'm the one calling the shots. Right now, I want you alive. Later, I won't."

"Let me guess, you want to kill me in front of Justin, so you can see him suffer?"

"Good guess. Have fun thinking about it for the next few hours." He smirked, walking back out of the room and shouting for Yvette to return.

She had tears in her eyes when she sat down in the chair minutes later, and finger marks on her wrist.

Despite the fact that Yvette wanted her dead, Gretchen couldn't help feeling sorry for her.

"No one you love should ever hurt you, Yvette," she said.

"He didn't." She rubbed her wrist and frowned.

"Then why are there marks on your arm?"

"I bumped into the kitchen counter."

"You're going to want to have a lot of those excuses in your repertoire, because if you and Boyd make it off base and to wherever he's promised you, you're going to have a lot of bruises to explain."

"Shut up, Gretchen. You have no idea what it's like to be with someone like him, and you never will. You're not good enough to attract a man of his caliber."

"I'm very thankful for that," she said sincerely, her eyelids so heavy she wanted to close them and let herself drift away for a while. She rolled her shoulders in the sockets, letting the pain drive her back to wakefulness. Her fingers brushed cool wood and the heavy fabric of her military jacket. When she was a kid, she'd dreamed of having one just like it. She'd open her father's closet and stare at his uniforms and imagine what it would be like to be a hero to the world.

He used to laugh when she asked him what it felt like, lifting her up and swinging her in circles, his pockets jingling with keys.

She blinked, that last word lodging in her brain.

Keys.

Had Boyd removed them from her pocket?

He'd taken the obvious set—the one she'd had hanging from her belt—but her father had taught her to keep an extra handcuff key hidden on her person. Just in case. She'd assumed he'd meant in case she lost a set. Now she thought he must have meant in case she was ever trussed to a chair with her own handcuffs.

She bent her arms, trying to maneuver them closer to her jacket pocket. The key was in a small slit she'd made in the fabric. It would be difficult to get, but if she could, she'd be able to free herself.

"Wiggling isn't going to help you," Yvette said.

"My shoulders are in agony. I'm trying to ease the pain."

"Don't worry. In a few hours, you won't be feeling a thing." She giggled, her angelic face obviously hiding a very dark soul.

"At least my eternity is going to be spent

in a much nicer place," she responded, wiggling again, using her hip to force the coat back against the spindles.

Her wrists felt like they'd snap, but she managed to get two fingers between the spindles. She used them to pull the coat taut and feel for the pocket.

There! She found the edge and shoved her fingers in between the fabric.

The key was there, the metal cool against her fingers.

"You know what your problem is, Gretchen?" Yvette asked, apparently oblivious to Gretchen's efforts to escape.

"What?"

"You think you're better than other people."

"What gave you that idea?" she asked, trying to keep the woman talking as she eased the key out of the pocket. She was sweating with fear, terrified she'd drop it, but she managed to get it out and close her fist around it.

"Boyd told me that's the way women like you are, and he's right."

"Like me? What am I like?"

"Career military. You get in and stay in and think you own the world because of it."

"I've only been in eight years."

"And you'd be in for eighty more if you

lived long enough. Which you won't." Yvette laughed. "You were so busy thinking you were better than me that you didn't notice I was collecting information."

"I guess I didn't." She felt the edges of the key, tried to get it in the right position. She might only get one shot. She didn't want to waste it.

"Well, I guess you've learned your lesson. It stinks being under lock and key, right? Now you know how my poor Boyd felt when he was in prison, don't you?"

"Yes."

"Are you thirsty? I mean, I know Boyd's right about the kind of person you are, but you were always nice to me. Even if you were faking it, I appreciate that."

"Water would be good," she lied. The thought of taking even a sip made her stomach heave.

"All right. I'll get you some. Kindness for kindness, right? That's what makes the world go round." She left the room, and Gretchen shoved the key into the lock, turned it.

She felt it click, and then she was free.

The cuffs were double locked, but she didn't open the second one. She was afraid they'd fall and make enough noise to bring Boyd running. She pocketed the key and positioned her hands so that only someone looking closely would know the cuff was open.

"Here you are." Yvette said, walking into the room with a water glass in hand, a straw poking out of it. "Don't worry. I didn't drug it. Boyd says you should be awake for the festivities."

"That's really nice of him," she muttered, taking a tiny sip of the water.

"You didn't drink much."

"I think I have a concussion. I don't feel very well. As matter of fact, I might get sick." That was the total truth, and she hoped to use it to her advantage.

"As in throw up?"

"That's what it feels like."

"You do look a little green."

"Maybe you could open the window and let some fresh air in. That might help." She knew from the setup of her apartment that Yvette's window would open. She also knew that a balcony stretched the entire length of the unit. If Yvette opened the window, all Gretchen would have to do was crawl through it.

"All right. I guess that's not going to hurt anything." She flipped the lock and cracked open the window.

"Can you open it a little more?"

"You're awfully demanding for someone who's on death row."

"Death row inmates get special privileges."

She opened it wider, and Gretchen winced as the vinyl pane squeaked.

"There," Yvette said. "Don't ask for anything else."

"I won't."

The doorbell rang, and Yvette jumped, whirling toward the bedroom door. "Who's that?"

"I have no idea. Maybe you should go check."

"It can't be your friends. They're off with their dogs, hunting for you. I can't wait until they find out you were here all along."

The doorbell rang again.

"Yvette!" Boyd appeared in the doorway. "Get your butt out there and open the door."

"But what if it's Justin?"

"It's not going to be. I set up cameras at the front of the building, remember? If he came back, I'd know it." He grabbed her arm and then pointed the gun at Gretchen.

"You scream or make noise and I'll kill whoever is at the door." With that, he yanked Yvette out of the room and shut the door.

TWELVE

Gretchen stood, her legs wobbly, her head fuzzy.

She was four floors up. She'd climbed rock walls higher than that, and on any other day, she wouldn't be worried about making it down the fire escape.

Today, though, her movements felt disjointed, her gait unsteady.

She could hear Yvette speaking to whoever was at the door.

Boyd had to be hiding somewhere close enough to take out anyone who tried to enter the apartment. Which meant Gretchen had a golden opportunity to get out. She had to hurry. She had to escape. She had to warn Justin. She had to get the team to the apartment building before Boyd fled.

But it was all she could do to make it to the window.

She managed it. Barely.

Once she was there, she leaned against the wall. Just for a second. Just to catch her breath.

Move it! She could almost hear her brothers shouting the orders. Or maybe it was Justin's voice.

She levered up, pushing her upper body through the window, her head swimming.

"You can do this," she muttered, pressing her hand against the siding, trying to gain enough momentum to slide through.

She closed her eyes, because the world was spinning.

Glass shattered, and for a second, she thought she'd broken the window. Then Yvette screamed, the sound raw and terrible.

Someone grabbed Gretchen from behind, yanking her back into the room, swinging her around, the cold barrel of a gun pressed to her cheek. She could see Justin in the doorway of the room, Quinn beside him. The dog lunged, growling and snarling.

"One wrong move, Justin, and I'll kill her," Boyd said.

"Don't do anything stupid," Justin replied.

"Stupid would be letting you capture me." Boyd shoved Gretchen forward, his grip tight on her upper arm.

"Let her go," Justin responded, Quinn growling deep in his throat, his teeth bared, his eyes on Boyd.

"Get out of the way," Boyd shouted, swinging the gun wildly, aiming it at Justin.

Gretchen tried to grab his arm, but her movements were slow and uncoordinated.

"I said move, Justin," Boyd screamed, the gun suddenly against her cheek again. "If you don't, I'll blow her beautiful face off."

"Calm down, Boyd," Justin said, stepping backward out of the room, his eyes locked on Gretchen.

She could see the fear in his eyes, but he wasn't panicked.

"It's going to be okay," he said calmly, and she believed him, because she believed *in* him. In the strength of his conviction and his faith, in his ability to think through the problem and come up with a solution.

And she believed in what he'd said, and what Henry had: that God was in control. That He would bring good to those who loved Him, and that no matter what happened, everything would be okay.

"Not if I don't get a car and a clear path off base," Boyd said. "You have three minutes to arrange that, Justin. You don't get it for me, and I'll shoot her in the knee. Every three minutes after that, I'll shoot her again. She's not just going to die, she's going to suffer."

"I'll get the ride," Justin said, taking another step back. He seemed to be moving toward the hallway. Or blocking Boyd's view of it.

"Good. Good," Boyd said. "That's what I like. Quick action. Come on, Gretchen. We're getting out of here." He nudged her forward, the gun slipping away from her face, and this time she was ready. She swung the handcuff, slamming it into his temple.

She expected the explosion of gunfire. Instead, she heard an angry snarl, and a large dog flew past, clamping his jaws on Boyd's leg and dragging him to the ground.

Not Quinn.

Beacon.

He must have come through the window.

She moved away from the writhing man and the dog. She'd seen Beacon the day he'd finally arrived from Afghanistan and been reunited with Isaac Goddard. He hadn't seemed vicious then. Now he was terrifying, Boyd's screams filling her ears.

She felt sick.

Really sick, and she stumbled to the couch, dropped down and pressed her head to her knees.

"Hey, it's okay. You're okay." Justin was beside her, his hand on her back, and she turned her head so she could see his face.

"Where's Yvette?"

"In cuffs out in the hall with Ava and Oliver."

"I can't believe she's been working with him all this time," she murmured, her head throbbing with every word.

"She had us all fooled." He felt her pulse, his fingers gentle on her wrist. "There's an ambulance on the way. We need to get you to the hospital."

"I'd rather stay here and see what Boyd has to say." She stood, and he grabbed her arm, holding her steady.

"I don't think standing is a good idea."

"I agree," Vanessa said, suddenly on Gretchen's other side. "Sit. Let me take a look. You've lost a lot of blood."

"Not enough to kill me," she said, sitting down again, because she still felt dizzy and off balance.

She tried not to wince as Vanessa probed the head wound, focusing instead on Justin and Isaac. They flanked Boyd, their dogs close beside them. He was cuffed, angry and as arrogant as ever.

"This isn't the end, Justin," he said, his face filled with rage. "I'm going to win. I always do."

"Not this time." Oliver stepped into the room, flashing his FBI badge at Boyd as he read him his Miranda rights, and Gretchen closed her eyes, trying to still the spinning world and anchor herself to the moment.

She was alive.

Justin was alive.

The team and their dogs were all okay.

And Boyd had been caught.

Finally. After months of hunting him, he'd been captured.

"Thank you, Lord," she whispered out loud, and someone squeezed her hand.

"I was just saying the same thing," Justin said, and she opened her eyes, realized she was on a gurney in the elevator.

She could hear someone crying, and she tried to sit up.

"Don't," Justin said, touching her shoulder and urging her to relax.

"Is that Portia?"

"No. She's still at the safe house, remember?" he asked, a note of concern in his voice.

"I got hit hard, but I haven't lost my memory. I just… Who's crying?" It wasn't a large elevator, and there was just enough room for the gurney, Justin and a medic.

None of them were crying.

She didn't think.

She touched her cheek. Just to be sure.

Justin smiled. "It's not you. In case you're wondering. Yvette is down in the lobby. She's been sobbing since I cut through the sliding glass door and took her into custody."

"I don't think many people would be happy about going to jail."

"It's not jail she's worried about," he said as the doors slid open.

Another medic was waiting in the lobby, and he helped roll the gurney out.

She thought he might be saying something to her, but she couldn't hear anything over Yvette's ear-piercing cries.

"Please!" she screamed. "Take me to the same prison. I just want to know we're close. Please, I'm begging you. Please."

"Someone shut her up!" Boyd shouted, his voice thundering through the lobby.

"Wow. Some lovebirds. They sound more

like alley cats," Gretchen said as she was wheeled outside.

"I was thinking the same," Justin replied.

"She's mentally ill," she said, because she was afraid she'd close her eyes and lose the opportunity. Yvette was sick and needed treatment.

She also needed to be behind bars.

"She's being transported to a high-security VA mental facility. That's why she's screaming," he explained. "She thought they were going to the base prison together."

"Is that where he's going?"

"No. We're transporting him directly to the federal prison he escaped from. Which I'm sure he knew would happen if he was caught. That's not what he told Yvette, though. He had her convinced that they'd be brought to our holding cell, and he'd escape again. With her, of course."

"Of course. She's going to be shocked when he turns on her during the trial, and you know he will. He was planning to abandon her and leave with me as his hostage. Meanwhile, she'd been dreaming of happily-ever-after. I shouldn't feel sorry for her. She might be mentally ill, but she did ask Boyd to kill me."

"I heard. I was outside the window when

you had that conversation with her. I wanted to break the glass and climb through, but I was afraid you'd be hurt before I could get both Boyd and Yvette under control. So I followed the plan and waited for Isaac to show. It was the worst three minutes of my life."

"Really?" she asked, reaching for his hand.

"Really. I've enjoyed having you as a partner, Gretchen. But I enjoy having you in my life even more."

"I feel the same way," she said, halfway thinking she was in a dream, because the world suddenly seemed made of soft edges and gentle slopes. Nothing hard or difficult or ugly.

"Good," he said. "Because I have some plans for after you've recovered."

"What kind of plans?"

"Moonlit walks, picnics after church, sitting beside the fire and listening to Portia gab with her friends while we just enjoy each other's company."

She smiled at that, because she could picture it happening. She could picture him—walking beside her for days and weeks and years to come. "That sounds like…"

"What?" he asked, touching her cheek and looking into her eyes.

"Like everything I could ever dream of."

"Good, because all of my dreams of the future suddenly have you in them. I love you, Gretchen. I need to say that now, because when Boyd had his gun to your cheek, I realized how much I would regret it if I never got the chance to say the words."

"I love you, too," she murmured, and he smiled.

"Sir?" one of the medics said, interrupting them. "Are you planning to ride along?"

"Am I?" Justin asked her.

Two words, but it seemed like more. It seemed like the most important question he'd ever asked.

"Can his dog come?" she asked, and the medic shrugged.

"I don't see a problem with it."

"Then yes," she responded, holding on to Justin's hand as she was rolled onto the ambulance, looking into his face as an IV was started. Memorizing the curl of his lashes and the curve of his lips. The fine lines near his eyes and the ones that bracketed his mouth. Filing every detail away, because this moment was the beginning of their journey together.

And she didn't want to forget any of it.

THIRTEEN

Thanksgiving

It had been a long time since Gretchen had been part of a big Thanksgiving celebration. She'd been back home for the holidays a few times over the past eight years, but her brothers were usually in distant locations, and Thanksgiving with her parents had been a quiet, intimate event. After years of hosting airmen and their families, that was the way her mother and father wanted it.

Gretchen didn't mind, but she'd missed the controlled chaos of large holiday gatherings. She'd always enjoyed the sounds of people chatting and laughing and enjoying each other's company. Growing up in a military family had meant moving a lot and leaving a lot behind, but it had also meant making strangers family.

Today, she was going back to those roots and to the sweetest of childhood memories. She couldn't wait.

She eyed herself in the mirror above her dresser, trying to ignore the deep circles beneath her eyes and the paleness of her skin. She'd spent nearly a week in the hospital after Boyd's attack, recovering from a fractured skull and a severe concussion. Even now, three weeks after the attack, she tired easily. She'd been on medical leave since the incident. Hopefully, she'd be cleared to work following the holidays. Once she finished her required time at the base, she could return to Minot.

Her phone rang as she grabbed her purse and stepped out of the bedroom. She glanced at the caller ID and smiled. Portia had come out of her shell since she'd returned from the safe house. She'd begun making friends at school, and she seemed happier, more content with her life. She enjoyed sharing stories about her day, telling Gretchen about her new friends.

Gretchen, for her part, had been happy for the distraction. Inactivity was boring, and she'd had too much of that while she was recovering.

"Hello?" She held the phone to her ear as

she walked down the hall and pushed the elevator button.

"Hi, Gretchen, it's Portia."

"I gathered that from the caller ID."

"Yeah. I had to say it, anyway. My mother drilled phone manners into my head."

"Are you missing her more today?" Gretchen asked, stepping onto the elevator.

"I miss her more every day," Portia replied, the sadness in her voice unmistakable.

"I'm sorry. I know it's hard to have Thanksgiving without her. Is there anything I can do to help?"

"Hurry up and get here? Dad said we can start the celebration once you've arrived."

"Am I late?" She glanced at her watch, worried that maybe she'd gotten confused. That had been a problem after the head injury. Although she'd been better during the past week. Clearer thinking. More focused.

According to the neurologist who was treating her, she still wasn't quite back to normal, but Gretchen could see the light at the end of the tunnel.

"No. It's still early. I just wanted to make sure you were coming. We invited the families of two of my friends from school. I don't want to act stupid in front of them."

"You're not stupid, so that would be impossible."

"I think you're forgetting that I was the anonymous blogger," Portia said with a sigh.

"Everyone makes mistakes."

"Not mistakes that almost get people they love killed. Anyway, Dad keeps saying I have to forgive myself, so I'm trying."

"Your dad is smart, too," Gretchen said.

"Would you say that if you weren't madly in love with him?" Portia giggled, obviously amused by her assessment of Gretchen and Justin's relationship.

"Madly, huh?"

"Would you call it something else?"

"I'd call it…wonderfully, beautifully, happily."

"The happy part sounds good. I love you both, and I want both of you to always be that. So, you're on the way?"

"Yes. Heading to my car now," she responded, stepping outside and crossing the parking lot.

"The doctor said you could drive, right? Because I don't want…" Her voice trailed off, but

Gretchen heard what she didn't say: that she didn't want Gretchen to get into an accident.

"Yes. I got cleared yesterday, and I'm thrilled. Maybe we can go Black Friday shopping tomorrow."

"No way. You've got to rest, and that won't be restful. I'll see you in a few." The teen disconnected, and Gretchen dropped her phone into her purse.

The sun was high and warm, the air chilly. Someone had a fire burning, the warm aroma drifting on the late-November air.

This wasn't supposed to be home, but lately it had felt like it. She'd expected to come to Canyon, do what she'd been assigned and return to Minot. She'd known she'd have to make a decision about her military career, but she hadn't imagined that she'd have something even bigger to decide.

Not that there *was* a decision.

She knew in her heart that a military career wasn't for her. Just like she knew deep down where it counted that right here was where she wanted to be. Close to Justin and Portia and all the people she'd come to care about. She'd spent some time with Ava these past few weeks, watching her train puppies for search and rescue. There were several civilian search and rescue teams in Texas, and she planned to join one after her honorable discharge from the air force.

She also planned to get her master's in forensic profiling. Eventually, she'd like to use trace evidence to make cases against criminal offenders.

She and Justin had discussed it over several dinners and over ice cream and over cups of coffee. Just thinking about the conversations they'd had and the time they'd spent together made her smile. She was still afraid of heartache. She was still worried that she might be shattered again one day.

But Justin was worth risking her heart.

And God was good.

He'd brought them through so many trials and challenges, and brought them to a place where they could meet and fall in love and make something beautiful out of the tragedy.

She pulled up in front of Justin's house, her heart pounding a little harder, her pulse beating happily in her veins. She could see people in the backyard, gathered under canopies that Justin had set in place the previous day. Adults. Kids. Teens. Dogs.

Family.

Not by blood or even by legality.

There was one thing she'd learned after spending a lifetime in the military. Sometimes family was a disparate group of people brought together by God.

She got out of the car, pulling her sweater a little tighter as a cool November breeze chased leaves across the grass.

A dog barked, and Quinn was suddenly there, nudging her hand with his nose, begging to be petted.

"Hey, boy. I bet you're having a fun day."

"He's having the time of his life," Justin responded, walking across the yard. Sun glinted in his hair and his flannel shirt pulled taut across his muscular shoulders, but it was his smile that made her heart swell with dreams she'd once thought were dead.

"And are you having fun?" she asked.

"More so now," he responded, pressing a quick, warm kiss to her lips. "You're beautiful, Gretchen."

"And you're a flatterer. But I'll accept the compliment." She took his hand, Quinn falling into step beside them as they headed around to the backyard.

She could see Linc Colson and his wife, Zoe, her little boy standing between them, and Linc's rottweiler lying in a warm patch of sunlight beside them. They were talking to Isaac and Vanessa, Beacon sitting next to Isaac and leaning against his leg.

"It's good to see them together," she said aloud.

"Who?" Justin asked, his palm warm against hers.

"Isaac and Beacon."

"I agree. Beacon is being retired from the military and is training to be Isaac's obedience and protection dog."

"I have a feeling Beacon will be good at any task." That reminded her of another German shepherd. "How's Scout doing?"

"Great. Westley has given all four shepherds some peace and quiet and rehab time, but they're getting back to work, and none of them seem the worse for wear."

"I'm glad. And I'm glad Boyd is where he belongs."

"And that Yvette is getting the treatment she needs," Justin added.

"Still no link between her and his crimes?"

"She helped him get on and off base. She helped him keep you prisoner. She did admit to planting the rose and the threatening note in her apartment to throw us off her track. More than likely, she'll be court-martialed and sent to a mental hospital for the rest of her life."

"Gretchen!" Portia called, racing across the yard, two teenage girls with her. "This is Lauren and Stacia. We're all on the school's yearbook committee. We're also starting a journalism club."

"Sounds like fun," Gretchen said, greeting each of the teens, happy and excited to see Portia connecting with people who had similar interests.

"It's going to be. We're going to do some investigative reporting on what they're putting into the cafeteria meals. We're thinking it's not actually food."

"Portia, don't get into trouble trying to prove that theory," Justin warned, and Portia laughed.

"Don't worry, Dad. I learned my lesson about digging up dirt. I'm going to keep my nose clean and do this the right way. Come on, girls. You can help me bring out that surprise I showed you earlier."

The girls hurried away, and Gretchen smiled. "I remember being that age."

"It wasn't that long ago."

"Long enough," she said. "Not that I'd ever

want to go back. It's hard making friends when you're the new kid."

"I hope she's happy," he said quietly, watching as Portia and her friends rushed into the house.

"She is. You're doing a great job, Justin. It's one of the things I love about you."

"So, there's more than one, huh?" He pulled her close, kissing her tenderly.

"Hey, none of that stuff," Maisy Lockwood called as she walked across the yard, a casserole dish in her hands. Chase McLear was beside her, his little girl in his arms. They made a beautiful family, his beagle, Queenie, trotting along behind.

"No?" Chase asked, leaning in to kiss her.

"I take back my protest." Maisy laughed, setting the casserole down on a long table filled with dishes. Portia had suggested a potluck, and Gretchen had agreed it would be the easiest way to feed a crowd.

Everyone who'd been invited had volunteered to bring something. Westley and Felicity had come with several dishes of food. Lieutenant Ethan Webb and his fiancée, Kendra, had offered to roast three turkeys. They were both standing beside the food table, Ethan's German shorthaired pointer, Titus, lying beneath it, the dog's long legs stretched out, his head resting on his front paws. Nick Donovan was on the other side of the table, his arm around his fiancée, Heidi Jenks, the base reporter. He was talking to Ethan, smiling as Annie, his bloodhound, nosed around near the table.

Obviously, she'd caught the scent of food.

Fortunately, the dogs were too well trained to snatch unattended food.

"It's pretty awesome, isn't it?" Justin whispered in her ear, and she didn't have to ask what. She knew. The team had been through so many trials and struggles. The return of the Red Rose Killer. The murder of Maisy's father, Chief Master Sergeant Clint Lockwood, and two dog trainers. The missing dogs. The Olio Crime Syndicate. Each person here had persevered and overcome.

There'd been sorrow, for sure. But there had also been joy.

She could hear it ringing across the yard—kids and adults laughing, conversation flowing. "It really is," she agreed.

"So, are you ready?" Isaac asked, walking toward them, Vanessa at his side.

She thought he meant for the turkey to be cut and the blessing to be said, but the other couples were gathering around. Kids and dogs and adults, forming a circle that she and Justin seemed to be in the center of.

"What's going on?" she asked, but then Portia stepped into the center, carrying a basket.

"We wanted to thank you for all you've done as a member of the team," Ava said. "You've become more than just a temporary transfer. You're a friend and a comrade."

"I feel the same about all of you," she admitted, surprised when Portia set the basket near her feet. A blanket lay over it, and she thought it might have wiggled. Quinn nosed in, his snout so close to the blanket Justin gave him the down command.

"What is it?" she asked, looking into Justin's eyes.

"Six months is a long time to be away from the people you love," he said. "We discussed it, and we decided that you needed something to remember us by."

"You make it sound like I'll be gone forever."

"Like I said," he responded, "six months is a long time. Go ahead. Take a look. Everyone on the team had a hand in helping choose your gift."

"Justin..." Her voice trailed off as she leaned down and lifted the blanket. A chubby puppy lay inside. Belly up and tail wagging, he looked like a red Lab—a breed Ava had said would be perfect for search and rescue work.

"His name is Winston," Portia said.

"He is the cutest puppy I've ever seen." She lifted Winston from the basket, smiling when he licked her chin.

"Since it looks like you're not *totally* in love with him," Portia said, sliding her arm around Gretchen's waist, "you can just say so, and we'll take him off your hands."

Gretchen laughed. "Nice try, kid. I adore him."

"I kind of knew you would. I named him Winston, because the first time I saw him, I thought he looked like a portly old man."

"A very cute portly old man," Gretchen agreed, teary eyed from surprise and pleasure.

She'd been given many gifts in her life, but this one, coming from so many people who cared, meant the most.

"Thank you all so much," she said.

"There's one more thing, Gretchen," Justin said. "But this one is just from me. To remember that I'm here for you, and that I always will be."

He took a box from his pocket and opened it.

"Justin," she breathed, not sure what she intended to say.

"I love you, Gretchen. You are everything I could ever want in a friend and life partner. I can't imagine my life without you. Will you marry me?"

The look in his eyes and on his face, the happiness and excitement and love there, filled her heart until there was no room for the past and its disappointments. There was only the future that they would create together.

"Of course!" she said, and he handed her the ring instead of sliding it on her finger.

"I hate to tell you this." Oliver chuckled. "But that's not the way it's done."

"Read it," Portia said, pointing to the words engraved inside the band.

In adversity, love blooms.

Gretchen's throat was tight, her eyes filled with tears.

"Yes," she managed to say, "it does."

Justin took the ring again, sliding it onto her finger this time. He kissed her then, deeply, passionately, their friends offering cheers and congratulations, the dogs barking and Annie baying.

Winston joined in, yipping happily and doing his best to lick the tears from Gretchen's face.

"He's already trying to make you feel better," Portia said, smiling at Justin. "You did good, Dad."

"I'm glad I have your approval," Justin said with a grin. "Now, how about we give thanks and eat?"

Gretchen set Winston back in the basket, linking hands with Justin and with Portia. One by one, they all did the same, standing in a circle beneath the pristine sky and thanking God for all the blessings they'd received. For the trouble and the triumph and the love they'd found along the way.

For His grace and His goodness in the dark times.

When they finished, Gretchen continued to hold Justin's hand, wrapped an arm around Portia and thanked Him again.

For faith, for family and for all the things that mattered most in life.

* * * * *

If you enjoyed the Military K-9 Unit series,
return to Canyon Air Force Base in
December 2018 for
Military K-9 Unit Christmas
by Laura Scott and Valerie Hansen.

Dear Reader,

What a blessing and joy to be able to end the Military K-9 Unit continuity! I love writing about K-9 teams, but the military angle was a new one for me. Military handlers and their dogs have a special bond, and I hope I've conveyed that in *Valiant Defender*. More important, I hope that I've offered you a satisfying ending to a wonderful series. Gretchen and Justin are compelling characters. Driven by their desire for justice, they pursue the Red Rose Killer with tenacity and faith. As you follow them on this journey, I pray that your faith will be strengthened and your hope renewed. Happy reading, my friend!

Blessings,
Shirlee McCoy